George Milner

Studies of Nature on the Coast of Arran

George Milner

Studies of Nature on the Coast of Arran

ISBN/EAN: 9783337030599

Printed in Europe, USA, Canada, Australia, Japan

Cover: Foto ©Andreas Hilbeck / pixelio.de

More available books at **www.hansebooks.com**

STUDIES OF NATURE

ON THE

COAST OF ARRAN

BY

GEORGE MILNER

[AUTHOR OF 'COUNTRY PLEASURES']

WITH ILLUSTRATIONS BY

W. NOEL JOHNSON

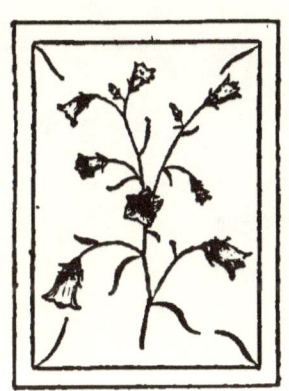

LONDON

LONGMANS, GREEN, AND CO.

AND NEW YORK : 15 EAST 16th STREET

1894

PREFACE

THE present volume may be regarded as, in some degree, a sequel or pendant to a previous work of the author's, published in 1879, and subsequently re-issued several times under the title of ' Country Pleasures.' The motive and plan of the two books are to a large extent the same. What is here presented is not the result of elaboration or afterthought, but is that which was written down at the time in journal-form when the impressions were fresh and vivid.

The writer can only expect that his unpretentious notes will prove interesting to those

who, like himself, care much for two things—
Nature and Literature—and who have given, or
are willing to give, to them devoted and affec-
tionate study. In 'Country Pleasures' a chapter
—that which deals with the month of August—
is concerned with the Island of Arran. In
'Studies of Nature' the subject is continued at
greater length.

It should be said with regard to the illustrations that they are an integral part of the work,
not merely random 'views in Arran,' but draw-
ings executed with loving care and conceived, as
far as may be, in the spirit of the writer, who
considers himself fortunate in having the colla-
boration of an artist at once so competent and
so sympathetic as Mr. W. Noel Johnson.

The names of the authors quoted are given in
a separate index, and a few Notes are appended.

CONTENTS

———

CHAPTER I

CHAPTER VI

CHAPTER VII

CHAPTER VIII

CHAPTER IX

CHAPTER X

CHAPTER XI

CHAPTER XII

CONTENTS ix

CHAPTER XIII

LIST OF ILLUSTRATIONS.

FULL-PAGE COPPERPLATES

ILLUSTRATIONS IN THE TEXT

STUDIES OF NATURE

ON THE

COAST OF ARRAN

———◆◇◆———

CHAPTER I

To make this earth, our hermitage,
A cheerful and a changeful page,
God's bright and intricate device
Of days and seasons doth suffice.
　　　R. L. STEVENSON, *The House Beautiful.*

CORRIE : *Saturday, August 2.*

IN Arran once more! And once more at the dear old hamlet of Corrie. To come here now means not only to attain peace and rest, much-needed and long sighed for, but also to welcome things familiar and already enshrined in the memory—the charm, in short, of change and freshness mingled with wont and custom.

B

And yet it was not without some feeling of loss that we bade good-bye to the old garden at home just when summer, sadly delayed, seemed to be breaking upon us. Hundreds of stately foxgloves, white and red and pale pink, were in full bloom on the sloping bed under the great hawthorn hedge; the creamy blossom of the elder was at its best; the first evening primroses were out; in the twilight at nine o'clock, the air was warmer than we had been accustomed to have it at noon, and the whole garden was filled with the heavy scent of musk and rose. All this was delightful enough, especially after the rigours of a nine-months' winter; but still, with the advent of August, there came back the old hunger for the mountains and the sea, and an idea haunted me like a superstition that with the first dip in the wave there would come a new life to both mind and body.

And here it is. The morning is still early, but I have had my accustomed plunge, and am sitting on the bench under the little window waiting for breakfast. No antidote could have more efficaciously ministered to a mind diseased by fume and fret and worry than this strange quiet—strange when contrasted with the vastness of our horizon. Although the sea is near enough for me to fling a stone into it from where I sit, there are cows feeding on the grass between me and the water, and the only sounds which rise out of all the great area over which the eye travels are the soft wash of the tide, and the crunching sound which the cattle make in cropping the short herbage. The wind is north-west, and, as is usual here, that turns everything into the brightest blue. The sea has many shades, but all of them are shades of blue, and the last is a line of deep sapphire under the opposite coast of Ayr. The islands are also blue, for their natural green is overborne; the sky is blue; and even the white clouds as they sail along seem to catch a tinge of the same colour.

And now, round the corner of the house, there comes an old friend, John Campbell, the 'Provost' of Corrie, as, with good-natured banter, he is usually called. Although he carries upon his shoulders the weight of more than eighty years, this last one seems to have added little to his burden. He steps forward as if he were pacing the unsteady deck of a lugger; and, putting his rough brown hand over his eyes, he looks round with an air of responsible authority upon the little hamlet and the wide sea as one who should say—'Stands Corrie where it did?' After salutations he opens out upon me quite at random, and as if we had parted not eleven months ago, but at sundown yesterday—The ministers nowadays are a' wrang in their theology; just blind leaders o' the blind, for not the one half o' them have been properly through the colleges. Why, with the Auld Testament in his haund he could pit them through their catechism hissel, and mak them a' flee before him

Dugald and his dog.

—puir creatures as they are. In his opinion the body politic, no less than the ecclesiastic, is in a parlous condition. These workin' folk have sent a' things tapsalteerie wi' their strikes and their high wages. When he was in the quarry he was weel content with his twa shillings a day; and the best mason among them a' got no more than three. An' what then; they were better off a lang sight than they are now.

When the old man goes slowly away, with steps that move like the minute hand of a clock, to take his accustomed outlook on the beach, another friend of the past comes up to me. He is not garrulous, but silent, and yet his face is full of language. He puts his shaggy and lion-coloured head upon my knee, and when his eye meets mine there is so much meaning in it that I know he recognises me as one who last year was his dead master's friend. This is Dugald's dog—Dugald the shepherd, who knew all the ins and outs of Corrie, and with whom I often

wandered along the burns and up the mountain-side. He died in the winter, or, as his old
mother put it to me with tears on her cheek,
'He's awa', sir, he's awa'.' And the dog—I
have heard his story already. It is that old
narrative of brute constancy and affection which
makes us ashamed for ourselves and our boasted
humanity. For months after his master's death
nothing would induce him to enter the house.
He rambled up and down the village picking up
his food where he could, sleeping on the hills
and refusing to be comforted. Only during the
last few weeks has he been prevailed upon to
return to the home which for him had lost its
light; and now, they tell me, he sleeps invari-
ably at the door of his late master's chamber.
As he trots away from me with his head hung
low, he turns and gazes wistfully north and
south along the village road and then up at the
mountains, as if he were looking for the well-
known form that will return to him no more.

Is it possible that his meeting with me has raised a train of association which leads him back dimly to the idea of his old companion, and arouses in him anew the affection which was so strong?

The dog and the man are now for me, both of them, treasures of the mind. Alas, poor Dugald! He was a gentle soul, kinder to all than to himself, and bravely risked his life on this coast, more than once, to save the lives of others. He sleeps by the side of a twin brother in the wild kirkyard at Sannox. In my visits to the Glen I shall not unfrequently turn aside to look at the shepherd's grave. Perhaps his dog will accompany me.

Sunday, August 3.

This morning we had a grey dawn and a grey sea. The water looked sometimes like polished metal—shining with a steely gleam in the transparent parts, and opaque in the shadows. In the evening the rain began; and while we sat in

the kirk vivid lightning played about the windows, and we could hear the thunder rolling
from peak to peak in Sannox Glen. The preacher
had a voice much too big for his building—big
enough, indeed, to have filled the dome of St.
Paul's; but once or twice his denunciations
were humorously drowned by the tones of the
thunder. The sea is now very heavy, and
flings an immense volume of water against, and
sometimes over, the great rock which is opposite
our door. It is quite dark except where a
glimmer of twilight, issuing from a break low
down in the sky, catches the tops of the waves
as they come hurrying and roaring onward to
the shore.

What a change is this from the evening
of yesterday. We were out fishing for whiting
with a deep-sea line when there came on one of
those marvellous sunsets which a man sees but
a few times in his life. The sea was a sheet of
molten glass and ready to mirror every tinge of

the sky. We were far enough from shore to be outside the shadow of the Island, and literally we floated in a sea of glory. The light came over the top of Suidhe-Fergus and, from where it struck the water, away for miles and miles the waves were of an inconceivable colour—an interchanging crimson, purple, blue, and green. Later, when the waves grew dark, the pomp was continued in the sky ; then the mountains became a wall of black, sharp in outline, but without further discrimination of form ; and, finally, the moon, rising late and just past the full, made a bridge of light from Ayrshire to Arran, and filled all the south-east with a radiance which was warm enough to be called golden. It is well, perhaps, that such days come but seldom. If they were a frequent visitation we should either have to veil our faces, like the leader of Israel, or repetition would dull the sense of beauty. In the meantime, when such a revelation does come it seems to speak to us as

a witness and a promise of that other life which
we look for, that second birth—

> Of all that is most beauteous—imaged there
>   In happier beauty; more pellucid streams,
> An ampler ether, a diviner air,
>   And fields invested with purpureal gleams.

CHAPTER II

They fancied the light air
That circled freshly in their forest dress
Made them to boys again. Happier that they
Slipped off their pack of duties, leagues behind.
.   .   .   .   Lords of this realm,
Bounded by dawn and sunset, and the day
Rounded by hours where each outdid the last
In miracles of pomp, we must be proud,
As if associates of the sylvan gods.

RALPH WALDO EMERSON, *The Adirondacs.*

CORRIE : *Monday, August* 4.

'WHEN you have nothing else to do,' says John Campbell, ' take to the boat '—that is good advice, and we often follow it here. Our own little shallop lies at the landing-slip, only a few yards from the door, and we get into it as easily as one puts on a pair of shoes. It is, indeed, our ' water-shoe,' and by means of it, during the hours between breakfast and early dinner, we saunter up and down the liquid plain ; or, keeping close in-shore, wander round the tiny creeks and coves. This is that judicious idleness which, if we can only attain unto it, is the proper object of a long vacation.

The best view of Corrie is to be gained from the water. Lying out, two or three hundred yards from the beach, we take in the whole place at a glance. Its elements are very simple. At the south end is the hotel, where the hostess, a model landlady, buxom, cheerful, motherly, dispenses hospitality with genial firmness. The tourist who can ' get in ' there either by grace or importunity, is a fortunate person, and many are the strange roosting-places which walking-men will put up with rather than be turned away from the door. At the north end is the school, a good building, and constructed, like the hotel, of dark sandstone. Between these two is the village, an irregular string of white, low-roofed cottages, with interspaces of garden and green brae-side, from end to end of which one can walk easily in a minute or two.

It is one of the peculiarities of a holiday that all the days at first seem singularly protracted; not, of course, by a sense of weariness, but by a change of circumstance, and the fulness of enjoyment. Days are mere arbitrary divisions, and Time is a figment—

> We live in deeds, not years ; in thoughts, not breaths ;
> In feelings, not in figures on a dial.

And so it seemed to me, floating aimlessly on the tide, as if weeks intervened between the present and my long journey from England. That journey is, indeed, a long one—most people regard it as a serious drawback against the advantages of Scotland—yet it may be taken as a pleasure. By the courteous arrangement of the railway company we have two or three compartments placed at our service, and pass, without intrusion, and without change either of

ourselves or our belongings, right on to the edge
of the quay on the Clyde at Ardrossan.   In this
way we are rid of anxiety and disturbance.
Disposing ourselves in one corner or another,
we bring out our books or our work and settle
down for a day's travel through the splendid
scenery of the Border.   After Skipton, we were
assured of a glorious day—bright and breezy,
full of life and motion, just the kind of weather
for the broad, bare, Yorkshire moorland which
lies between Penyghent and Ingleborough.
There had been heavy rain in the early morning, and the streams were all swollen—dark in
the deep places, light brown where broken by
the rocks.   In this limestone country all the
rivers are short and swift, leaping down the
precipitous ledge on the hillside, or hurrying
along some narrow and gloomy rift.   Further
on, when we come into Westmoreland, where
the lime changes to sand, the rivers are wide,
slow, 'full-fed,' and sweep majestically across

the fertile plain, with romantic hills on either side. Of all the places we pass, Appleby, with its fine church, its grey clustering houses, and its thick woods, tempts me most to linger, and I make a mental note—' come and stay at Appleby upon the first available opportunity.' At Carlisle we catch a glimpse of Skiddaw; and, after passing Dumfries, we plunge again into a romantic country, like that which we have left on the other side of the Solway. The landscapes are those of the Scottish Ballads. They are romantic, as I have just said. But romantic is a vague word. I mean by it, however, a country not dependent for its effect either upon cultivated richness or upon mountain sternness. A country of glens, and crags, and rivers, and pastoral sweetness, whose eminences are hills rather than mountains. I was reminded of this by passing a station bearing the name of Kirkconnel. We were not quite sure that these were the real Braes of

Kirtle; but, as we hurry past, we catch a
glimpse by the river-side of just such a pensive
glade as that on which the incomparable Helen
might have received the dart which was intended for her lover; and, thereafter, for the
rest of the journey, the sobbing cadences of the
old ballad go murmuring through the mind, or
break into half-audible song with the rumble
of the train for accompaniment.   Strange con-
fluence of the ancient and the new !—

> I wish I were where Helen lies !
> For night and day on me she cries ;
> I wish I were where Helen lies,
> On fair Kirkconnel Lea !
>
> O Helen fair, beyond compare !
> I'll weave a garland o' thy hair,
> And wear the same for ever mair,
> Until the day I dee.
>
> I wish my grave were growing green,
> A winding-sheet about my een,
> And I in Helen's arms lying
> On fair Kirkconnel Lea !

At Mauchline the clouded Arran looms in
the West, and I remember with much interest

that this is the view which Burns must have seen familiarly out of his Ayrshire home. One cannot but wonder that a prospect, so startling and lovely by turns as this is, should have left little or no mark upon his poetry. But then he lived before the mountain-passion had been developed. From this point to the time when we land at Brodick we keep our eyes on the ever-nearing Island. As usual, it presents a grand spectacle, being transfigured and possessed by the agencies of light and cloud. It is a delight therefore to think that we are to live for a time upon its margin.

Wednesday, August 6.

Wind in the North-East. Cold and rainy. The sea a greyish green, flecked with a few white waves, which look like gulls in the distance. Over the landing-slip a dozen real gulls are hovering just now, as they usually are. The eye is fascinated by their motion—graceful,

C

deliberate, and consummately adapted to its object. With what ease they float and rise, fall and turn, uttering all the while their plaintive and half-human cry! Some of their gyrations are evidently intended for exercise or for simple pleasure; but their main purpose is, of course, to pick up such stray scraps of food as are found lying about the rocks. The fishermen sit here in the afternoons, baiting their long night-lines, and leave odds and ends behind them. Then there are eels, and dog-fish, and other rejected creatures thrown back into the water, which the gulls appropriate; and sometimes their quick eyes detect the young 'saith' swimming in the shallow water over the grey slabs, and, sweeping down swiftly, they snatch them out with great dexterity. They are very tame; and frequently we see one of them sitting like a duck close to the shore for a long time. Probably they are shrewd enough to know that nobody on the Island carries a gun except the

W Noel Johnson, Del.   Walker & Boutall Ph Sc

"Wot's the odds so long's yer 'appy."

duke and his own people, and that consequently
there are no random shots fired by what Wen-
dell Holmes calls the 'gunning idiot.' Other
live creatures frequent the shore. There are
the jackdaws which roost in the rocks behind
the village and come down to the water's edge
for something dainty which they find there.
The people warn us not to leave coin or
jeweller's work about our tables, as the daws
sometimes come indoors and make off with such
small valuables. Then there is the restless but
delightful pied wagtail. He divides his time
between the garden and the beach, and is
equally at home with either. If I leave the
birds, I must mention first the sheep and lambs
—the latter looking like woolly toys—which
just now are leading a happy existence on the
sedgy strip of green which joins the road on the
side nearest the sea; and next, the Boy—
the typical boy of the village who is always to
the front, dabbling in the pools, or lying in the

boats, or hanging over the quay. He is a very small, brown, barefooted, and amphibious creature. On a survey of him you would say that he was three-fourths trousers, and nearly one-fourth blue bonnet. Both the trousers and the bonnet appear to have been originally the property of some much larger person. An adaptive ingenuity, however, has brought them, more or less, into harmony with his necessities. Probably he knows that his attire is not of a fashionable character ; but we can imagine him saying, as our facetious member puts it, ' What's the odds, so long's you're happy ? '

CHAPTER III

Trust me, 'tis something to be cast
Face to face with one's Self at last,

. . . . . .

And to be set down on one's own two feet
So nigh to the great warm heart of God,
You almost seem to feel it beat
Down from the sunshine and up from the sod ;
To be compelled, as it were, to notice
All the beautiful changes and chances
Through which the landscape flits and glances,
And to see how the face of common day
Is written all over with tender histories,
When you study it that intenser way
In which a lover looks at his mistress.

JAMES RUSSELL LOWELL. *Pictures from Appledore.*

CORRIE : *Thursday, August 7.*

THREE steamers touch at Corrie every day, the
Glen Rosa, the *Guinevere,* and the *Sheila,* going
on to Brodick, and Lamlash, and returning in

the afternoon. If we want a change we go
out in the ferry-boat, jump on to one of these
passing steamers, and get a delightful sail of
twenty miles or so. Sometimes we do this for
the sake of the sail only. We have a pleasant
lounge on deck, and come back without landing.
On hot afternoons this is a sensible way of
taking the *siesta* ; and one smokes, and another
reads, and another sketches. It is healthier
and ever so much better than the traditional
slumber in an arm-chair. But to-day we landed
at Lamlash and walked home. The wind was
in our favourite north-west, fresh but not cold ;
the sky blue and breezy, the sea ever changing
but ever beautiful. As we scud along by the
shore we sit so that our faces are turned towards
Arran. Nothing else is so interesting. The
eye, never wearied, runs again and again along
the wonderful mountain-line just as on some
ancient melody the ear will dwell for a hundred
times without sense of satiety. The visible ridge

begins northwards with Cioch-na-h'oighe at the
mouth of Sannox Glen ; then, sailing southward,
comes Am Binnien which looks over Corrie;
then Goatfell behind the bold shoulder of
Maoldon ; and, as the steamer swirls into Brodick
Bay, we see the softer outlines behind Glen
Cloy. Further on, the mountains are hidden
by the lofty coast line ; but just before we reach
Lamlash, there is a break in the barrier and
through it we catch a momentary glimpse of
Ben Gnuish, one of the finest hills in the island.
The Bay of Lamlash forms a magnificent
harbour, the Holy Island running across for
quite two-thirds of the distance between one
horn and the other, and rising to a height of
more than a thousand feet. This island has a
legendary interest. It is said to have been the
residence of St. Molios, an Irish abbot and
bishop, in the sixth century, and of Nicolas, a
Norwegian hermit, six centuries later. It rises
abruptly from the water, and is a striking and

picturesque object, whether seen from the land or from the sea.

Lamlash has a character of its own. It is neither so rugged as Corrie, nor so soft and beautiful as Brodick. Corrie is a nest at the mountain-foot, and there is little more than standing-room for its houses; the sea breaks roughly upon it, its air is the most bracing in Arran, it has no pretensions, and its frequenters have none. Brodick lies in a basin and, although but six or seven miles away, its climate is perceptibly softer. It is also under the shadow of a castle, and plumes itself upon the frequent patronage of a duke. Lamlash has a sheltered situation, and a mild climate also; but then it lives in the presence of the duke's factor, and not in that of the duke. It is plebeian, therefore, and in consequence is mildly snubbed by the aristocratic Brodick. It is a right pleasant place, however, and has a clean and homely look. The whitewashed houses run for perhaps half a mile along the Bay, with a broad green sward in front of them. At one point behind this line a few cottages huddle snugly together, with a smithy and some rural workshops among them, and make a cheerful

Lamlash

kind of hamlet on the edge of the green country. Beyond this a lane, shaded by tall trees and having a burn on each side, makes towards the hills. On the pier there is always a little stir, steamers touch frequently, and there is a good deal of boating. The bare-legged lads of the

village fish there all the day long in the deep
water. They are a sharp-witted race, keen of
feature, and quick of speech. 'Johnnie,' said
one of them to another as I stood there,
'Johnnie, ye've got a bigger fish noo than ever
ye had in your life before.' Turning round to
look at the great catch, I heard the young
rascals laughing consumedly. It was myself
who had been caught. To get the big hook
out of my tweed trousers was a long and somewhat trying operation. Among the characters
of Lamlash is Sandy M'Glosher. Sandy is a
fisherman and a boatman, and has a thriving
trade. All through the winter months he fishes
hard, and never tastes whisky; but as soon as
summer brings visitors, Sandy is sober no more.
It is whisky, whisky, all the day long. Last
night, after eleven o'clock, a splash in the water
was heard by a casual passer-by. Sandy had
rolled off the pier, and had a narrow escape of
his life. He was drawn in by one foot—a mere

floating log. 'Well, Sandy,' we said to him, 'it was well you were picked up last night.'

'Oh, don't believe it, gentlemen, don't believe it. I was just bathing.'

' And at midnight, Sandy ? '

' What for no ? It's a guid thing bathing, at all hours.'

' And with your clothes on, Sandy ? '

' What for no ? I have na' always just the time to tak' aff ma' claes when I want to bathe.'

Poor Sandy ! Have a care, or some day you will bathe after this fashion once too often, and then there will be sore weeping among the five weans who will be waiting for you at home.

In the evening we began our journey homeward. The road leaves the coast and runs across the promontory which ends in Clachland Point, and which separates the Bay of Lamlash from that of Brodick. As we climb slowly towards the summit-level we turn often to gaze

at the Holy Island which fronts us, looking
east—

A precious stone set in the silver sea.

It would always be worth while to make a
journey to Lamlash if only for the sake of seeing
the Holy Island under its various aspects. I
cannot remember anything at all like it elsewhere. It is unique. Seen from this road it
presents—as indeed from many other points—
an appearance which can only be described as
startling—a thing not to be expected in the
ordinary course of natural scenery. Startling
in its beauty, for the shores in this evening light
rise soft and green from a placid sea; startling
in its grandeur, for beyond the narrow and
verdant margin the rocks tower to a great
height, precipitous and dark. When this view
is lost we begin the descent towards Brodick, a
wide moorland in the foreground and the Goatfell range behind. It is a pleasant road. Many
little burns come wimpling through the heather,

and are crossed by small bridges. On each of these it seems natural to pause, for a bridge is always a place to linger upon, and over each low and mossy parapet we get a peep into some tiny glen, down which the water glances between

Holy Island

banks that are adorned by the foxglove, the fern, and the wild rose. By the roadside we notice the campion, a spring flower still in bloom; the bramble, in flower also, though by this time its fruit should almost be ripe; the sweet-scented woodruff, and the jewelled forget-me-not.

We shorten our walk two miles by crossing Brodick Bay in a boat. The waves are heavy, and we have to pull hard to reach the old quay under the castle; but the splendour of sunset is upon us, and the water, as it drips from the rising oar, is the colour of red wine. The dark is falling as we come in sight of Corrie. The night clouds are already enfolding the peak of Goatfell, and there is a wild look about the White Water which can still be seen tumbling down its front.

CHAPTER IV

Over our manhood bend the skies;
  Against our fallen and traitor lives
The great winds utter prophecies;
  With our faint hearts the mountain strives.

Its arms outstretched, the Druid wood
  Waits with its benedicite;
And to our age's drowsy blood
  Still shouts the inspiring sea.

JAMES RUSSELL LOWELL. *The Vision of Sir Launfal.*

CORRIE : *Friday, August* 8.

THE present month of August is dowered with two moons; or perhaps I had better say, with a moon twice at the full. This is a clear gain to us, and one which we greatly appreciate. On the second night of our stay here we saw, as I have already recorded, the broad golden disk—a perfect circle—riding in the south; and we shall see it once more before we leave. How much those people lose who do not care to wait upon the moon. It is as though one should miss half the world. Night after night now we watch its waning beauty—no, not its waning beauty, but its beauty as it wanes. I say this because the moon is never more lovely than at this time, and diminution of size only seems to give increase to a certain strange and weird quality which appertains to it when the final quarter is approaching. I suppose I shall be told that all this is association. Be it so: I merely record my impressions.

Last night, after our long walk from Lamlash, I opened the door about eleven o'clock and looked out. The hamlet was at rest, the twinkling lights were all extinguished, and the last fisherman had gone from the rocks. There was no sound of voices, no footfall, only a low babble of waves along the shore. I was alone with the sea and the sky. The sky was a deep

dark blue, the brighter stars were visible, and
the moon hung, as it seemed, near the earth,
forward, and away from the firmament. And
the sea, what was that like? After looking at
it long, I said—it is mother-of-pearl. Only that
can describe its evanescent tint—a shimmering
and interchanging mixture of green and blue
and silver.

To-day has been cloudy, and the evening
good for deep-sea fishing. As we pulled out to
our moorings we observed how distinct were the
details of form away in the distant islands—
more distinct than they often are when the sky
is bright and clear. About half a mile from the
shore we rattle out the anchor, and the boys
begin to fish. I take a line too; but I fear it
is more than half pretence. Fishing does not
come to me by nature, sea-fishing less than any
other; and so, although I lean over the boat-
side with my finger on the cord, I am by no
means anxious for a bite. If a fish comes, of

D

course you must pull him in ; and then, there
is that ugly half minute while you are getting
the hook out of his throat, and during which
he looks at you with more intelligence than
you care to notice. And so I am better

Sea Fishing

pleased if the fish will just let me alone, and
go on disporting themselves on the brave sea
· bottom.

Perhaps it is this *sea*-fishing which does not
suit me. After all, when I come to remember it, the master of the craft himself had

evidently no love for angling in salt water. You know what he says in the 'Angler's Song':

> I care not, I, to fish in seas—
> Fresh rivers best my mind do please,
> Whose sweet calm course I contemplate,
> And seek in life to imitate.

I must try the rivers. I must cultivate with more assiduity a disposition of contentedness and patience, and apply myself to the rod, and court the Corrie Burn where it lingers in those deep rock-pools shaded by birch and hazel. It would be worth while to become, even now, an unquestioned angler, if only for the privilege of appropriating and putting into one's mouth that delightful piece of railing which the gentle Izaak has included in his first chapter: 'There are many men that are by others taken to be serious grave men, which we contemn and pitie; men of sowre complexions; mony-getting men, that spend all their time first in getting, and next in anxious care to keep it:

men that are condemn'd to be rich, and alwayes discontented or busie. For these poor-rich men, wee Anglers pitie them, and stand in no need to borrow their thoughts to think ourselves happie.'

While these reminiscences are running through my head I am looking round on what is above and beneath me. The sea is scarcely ruffled, but it swings to and fro with large smooth waves. Lying at this distance from the shore, and with your eye close to the water, how vast the liquid plain appears! The sky is vast also. There is no brilliant colour to-night. The clouds are grey, or only touched very faintly with amber and green; but they cover the sky in bands and ranges whose number seems infinite, and the effect produced is that of boundlessness and airy space. Perhaps this feeling is increased by the sight of the birds as they sail slowly round us, rising sometimes to a great height and then sweeping down till they touch the water. They are fishing like ourselves.

By this time we have got a fair complement of small and delicate whiting lying in the bottom of the boat, and, suddenly, my eldest boy gives an unsportsman-like shout. He has caught a lusty haddock, and looks round triumphantly at the catchers of tiny whiting. His pre-eminence, however, is of short duration. A younger brother begins to scream, and pulls frantically at his line. There is a rush, and it is as much as I can do to keep the boat from being overturned. I expect he has got into a tangle of seaweed or caught somebody else's lead, and beg him to be calm and to seat himself; but he turns round upon me with as much of scorn as he dares to show, and keeps on pulling with tremendous excitement, and an eye that seems as if it would pierce the green water to its furthest depths. And there at last, sure enough, is the head of a great fish above

the waves, a fish that had no business to take
so small a hook—the fool of his race, I suppose.
It is no easy matter to land him, and just at
the critical moment the line breaks ; but our
young fisherman makes a bold dart—he only
just missed joining the fish in the water—and
dexterously slips his hands under the open
gills.   It is my turn now ; and, seeing what is
almost sure to happen, I seize boy and fish at
once and fling them both into the bottom of the
boat.

When we have settled down and have time
to look round we find that we have caught
ι, fine specimen of that voracious rascal, the
herring-hake.   He is about three feet long and
not unlike the salmon in colour.   He lashes
about wildly among the whiting, and for a few
minutes we have to hold him down.   The small
fry must have wondered much what Triton it
was that had come amongst them.

And now, lads, pull home ; the larder is

replenished with fish at any rate—pull home,
and sing to the stroke—

> I cuist my line in Largo Bay,
>   And fishes I catch'd nine ;
> 'Twas three to boil and three to fry,
>   And three to bait the line.
> The boatie rows, the boatie rows,
>   The boatie rows fu' weel ;
> And muckle luck attend the boat,
>   The merlin and the creel.

A proud boy was Master Arthur as he
walked heroically up from the creek, at the
head of the procession, with the great herring-
hake hanging over his shoulder and all the
youth of Corrie looking on. We larger boys
walked modestly after him, bearing the diminu-
tive whiting.

CHAPTER V

If thou art worn and hard beset
With sorrows, that thou wouldst forget,
If thou wouldst read a lesson, that will keep
Thy heart from fainting and thy soul from sleep,
Go to the woods and hills !—No tears
Dim the sweet look that Nature wears.
                    LONGFELLOW, *Sunrise on the Hills.*

CORRIE : *Saturday, August* 9.

THE wind this morning is due north—blowing, that is, right from the Highlands. Between this place and Cape Wrath over what a wild country it travels, bringing messages to me here, on the sea-shore at Corrie, from many a far-off and yet well-known Ben and Loch—from Nevis and Cruachan, from Leven and Etive and Awe.

The early bath, though cold, has been a fine

and invigorating thing. How could it be otherwise in such clear, living, tumbling water as
that is which comes with this north wind? As
I lay on the waves I could see the moon still
shining faintly in the blue, and the purple crest
of Am Binnein peering at me over the green
foreland. Wet or fine, hot or cold, we never
miss the morning plunge. For that the law
was promulgated on the first day of our arrival,
and it is not to be broken. We may take a
bath at noon, for pure luxury, in that warm and
sandy cove which we have discovered on the
shore about half a mile towards Brodick, and
into which we can pull with the boat, but that
is not to excuse the Spartan dip among the
rocks opposite the door here. It is an advan-
tage in such bathing that the preliminary
costume may be of the scantiest character. The
figures that are to be seen furtively crossing the
road each morning before breakfast are grotesque,
if not ridiculous. My æsthetic friend says they

present him with pictures of the ignoble savage
and his young barbarians all at play; but we
can afford to disregard his gibes. When the
slender integuments are laid aside Nature asserts
herself; it is then seen that simplicity is beauty
and that freedom is grace. Seriously, who will
show me the *genus homo* in finer form than that
which is to be seen when the lithe and shapely
limbs of a young lad are cleaving the transparent waves? It seems then as if we were
almost as clearly intended to swim as is the bird
to fly.

This early bathing has already afforded us
several amusing episodes. Here is one of them.
It is the vice of our young swimmers to stand
shivering on the brink till the skin has cooled
down. To remedy this I offer a reward to the
one who is first in the water. They start fair
from the door and reach the edge together.
Then it becomes apparent that the question is
simply who can most quickly slip away from the

slough of his shirt.   But the next day each mother's son of them tries to steal a march upon the others.   There has been rain in the night, the sward is slippery, and as they run helter-skelter down the bank one falls and the rest roll over him.   It is then seen that though they have overcoats on their shoulders they are shirtless—naked as when they were born, but striped with the wet soil.   Peals of derisive laughter are heard from the cottage as they pick themselves up, and, leaving the coats on the ground, rush down and hide themselves in the creek.

I have not heard what are the chemical constituents of the salt water at Corrie.   It is said to be wonderfully efficacious in strengthening feeble limbs.   Certainly it is more pungent than any water I have had experience of.   The old Provost, who knows everything and has everything under his charge, is delighted with our persistency in bathing.   'It's the right thing ye'r doin', maun, just the right thing ye'r doin'; for it's graund water—graund to douk in and graund to drink o'. Tak' a cup o' it every mornin' fastin' an' ye'll never dee at all—ye'll just live on an' renew ye'rsell like the eagles.'

Although our boat is not a large one, yet, with a few stones in her for ballast, she will carry a small lug-sail, and we had set to-day apart for a short cruise. Willie MacNiven, however (Willie is the cheeriest and handsomest boatman in Corrie), shakes his head and says we must content ourselves on shore, for the wind as it is now would blow us clean off the water. Having waited till evening we then determined to try the mountains, and decide on Cioch-na-h'oighe for the sake of seeing again the wild river of rocks up in the high hollow. In the village there are signs of Saturday night. The three trading smacks in the little harbour are having their decks scrubbed; the brown fishing nets are hung up on the trestles—there

is no more fishing till Monday—and old Robert
Campbell, the Provost's elder brother, is 'penk-
ing' with a hammer at his boat, which he has
got turned over on the beach. Robert is ninety,
if not more; yet he is still hale and strong, and
is always in the open air clinging to the rocks
like a limpet; but his eyes are very dim, and '
when he speaks the sound of his voice is faint
and strange and like that of a man talking to
you from afar off. He would make an excellent study for the Ancient Mariner or for Mr.
Gilbert's seaman of the *Nancy Bell.*

We turn from the sea, about half way on
the road to Sannox, by a path which leads past
a little waterfall and makes straight for the
Cioch. When we reach what is called the old
sea-level the walking becomes a little rough,
and the girls must needs gather up their skirts
and make all 'taut,' as the sailors say. The
boulders lie thickly about, and are masked with
heather and moss. In other places it is wet,

but by careful watching you soon come to find
the narrow tracks that are made by the shepherds and their sheep, and these are generally
dry.   We observe that every important water-
course is marked by a birch wood.   Strange
places are these—dim and dark, or lighted only
by a green glimmer.   The trees are low—you
must often stoop to pass under them—and are
much withered beneath, the verdant branches
being only those next the sky.   All the ground
is strewn with fallen twigs, which snap and
crack under your feet.   These dry and twisted
birch stems are singularly like serpents ; and,
as we know that the adder is not uncommon in
Arran, we frequently get a slight shock of alarm.
Nearer the shore many of the trees are large,
but at the same time gnarled and hollow.
Whenever I come into these groves by the sea
I bethink me of the wild woods of Broceliande
and of the lissome and snakelike Vivien lying
at Merlin's feet.

When we get into open ground we are on the shoulder of the mountain, and begin to climb steeply by the side of the stream which comes down from the corrie. The water is colourless, and falls over ledges of light grey rock—light enough almost to be called white. This is the form which the cataract usually takes among these hills. We see it at the White Water under Goatfell and elsewhere—a series of bare, steep slopes of granite, lying on the open mountain side, exposed to sun and wind, and along which the flood, singularly limpid, slides or rolls, as the case may be. At the head of this fall we pause and look upon a glorious prospect. The sun is setting and the north wind, blowing all day, has removed every trace of mist or cloud. The Frith of Clyde is all beneath us. There is Inch Marnock and Bute and the two Cumbraes. On the larger of these we can see distinctly the white houses in Milport. Northward there is Loch Striven and the hills of Argyle, and, in the far distance, we can even make out Ben Lomond—quite fifty miles away as the crow flies. The only sound we hear is that of the falling water near us, and the distant boom of the sea. Before such a scene the mind naturally takes a tone of reverence and of elevated tranquillity. Things are transfigured. The earth is not earthly: it appears to hang or float in the sky like an airy band of cloud, while the sea, being flat and solid blue, seems more substantial than the land itself. Readers of Wordsworth will know to what passage I should, under such circumstances, be most likely to revert :

> The broad sun
> Is sinking down in its tranquillity ;
> The gentleness of heaven is on the sea :
> Listen ! the mighty Being is awake,
> And doth with His eternal motion make
> A sound like thunder—everlastingly.

Nor, when I looked round upon one of my young companions, did what follows in the same sonnet seem to me inappropriate :

Cioch na H'eighe and the Devils Punch Bowl.

Dear child! dear girl! that walkest with me here,
If thou appear'st untouched by solemn thought,
Thy nature is not therefore less divine :
Thou liest in Abraham's bosom all the year ;
And worshipp'st at the Temple's inner shrine,
God being with thee when we know it not.

From this point we climbed rapidly into the corrie. Cioch-na-h'oighe is a hollow mountain, the summit of which is a narrow, jagged, and semicircular ridge. At the north-eastern corner this ridge ends in a peak which is one of the wonders of the island. Looked at from below, it changes its shape, according to your position, in a marvellous way. Sometimes it is a horn, curving over beyond its base; sometimes a pyramid, like a lesser Matterhorn, detached from the rest of the mountain; and again it takes that form from which it derives its name —the maiden's breast. The great hollow or corrie is immediately under the ridge. It is dry, but if it held water it would remind you strongly of the Welsh tarn, Llyn Idwal. Up on the right there is even a cleft in the ridge,

E

dark and awful, which is quite a repetition of the well-known Twll-Dhu, or Devil's Kitchen, which, looking up from Idwal, you see on the side of the Glydr Vawr. Even here there are flowers. As we came up we saw the tormentil, the harebell, and the blue milkwort; but we did not expect to find any blossom so high as this. But, sure enough, in a green plot, under the very shadow of the crags, we come upon quite a little garden of foxgloves. They are stunted, and pale in colour, but beautiful when seen in such a place.

We turn now to that scene which is the special object of our visit, and which it is impossible to describe. Two or three years ago a great waterspout broke on the ridge and poured a tremendous flood down the mountain. What that flood must have been we see from what is around us. Along its course the very bones of the hill, as it were, are laid bare; rocks, many tons in weight, have been hurled from their beds, and have evidently crashed and bounded over each other. You can still see how the ground has been flattened, or dragged, or ploughed up by what went over it; and how, in some cases, a rock larger than usual has stopped in its headlong course and then divided the stream of smaller blocks. In one place I took a measurement, and found that the width of the torrent must have been fifty yards. It would not be easy to find a scene of wilder confusion, or a more striking evidence of what may be done by the uncontrollable forces of Nature.

The twilight pursued us fast as we ran, sometimes breast-high in bracken and heather, down into Sannox Glen. When we reached the village it was almost dark, but the masts of the boats in the harbour were sharp and clear against an orange sky in the north.

CHAPTER VI

There comes a murmur from the shore,
And in the place two fair streams are,
Drawn from the purple hills afar,
Drawn down unto the restless sea.
WILLIAM MORRIS, *The Life and Death of Jason.*

CORRIE : *Tuesday, August* 12.

THIS week, so far, we have had warmer
weather. On Sunday service was held at
Sannox Kirk, with all the windows open and
half the congregation sitting on the grass outside. This is regarded by many as a convenient
arrangement. Those who took their places in
the open air had the manse garden, and the
sea, and the mountains, and the burn all in
sight; and if they found the discourse too
tedious for them, they might wander in search
of sermons elsewhere, and return in time for
the blessing. But for my part, finding it not a

whit too long, I listened to the whole. It was a
sweet and simple homily from an old Highland
preacher, whose mind seemed to be well in tune
with all the beauty around him. There was
edification even in looking at him. His face
had evidently been harsh once, but increasing
years appeared to have softened its expression,
as they had also probably relaxed the sterner
lines of his Scottish theology. I shall always
remember with pleasure how in artless phrases
he described us, the summer visitants, as children sent forth for a space to play among the
hills, in the presence and under the approving
smile of the great Father. When he said this
I could not help reverting to that pleasant
picture with which the ' The Ancient Mariner '
closes, where all the people

> Walk together to the kirk,
> And all together pray,
> While each to his great Father bends,
> Old men, and babes, and loving friends,
> And youths and maidens gay !

This is just what we see at Corrie—a goodly company walking together in the bright morning air along the shore, without haste, cheerful and yet sedate; and then sitting together in the little house of prayer with no distinctions of age or rank. And what strikes one most is that *all* are there; not the visitors only, but the rough lads of the village and the hard-faced boatmen; the Provost and the shoemaker; the 'braw' lassie and the old wife—you recognise them all with some surprise as they slowly enter, clad in their blue pilot suits and home-spun gowns.

To-day, for the sake of change, we have been to Loch Ranza. The younger folk were anxious for an early start. 'Let us have the whole long day,' they said; and so it was proposed that we should set out at six, and get the walk over before breakfast. Finally, however, more moderate counsel prevailed, and about nine o'clock we marched through the village, picking up friends here and there until our party numbered nearly twenty. A little beyond the school-house there is a certain boulder standing on the shore. It is a strange piece of work, singular in shape and huge in size. Frost, or some other agent, has sent a rift right through it, and the upper portion has slid forward a foot or so. If you stand with your back against it and look southward you get the best possible view of Corrie—a view which would always tempt you to take out pencil and sketch-book.

There is the curved margin of the beach; the winding high-road; the long, picturesque group of houses, backed from this point by a grove of trees; and, in the far distance, where the sea makes its horizon line, the bold form of Holy Island. Here we wait to see if there are any stragglers, and then set forward upon our journey. In such a company the high spirits of the young people are infectious, and we sober pilgrims not unfrequently find ourselves joining in some wild and guttural Scottish chorus, which echoes again and again from the over-hanging rocks by the shore. A stranger would hardly have known what to make of a grave and reverend person shouting, at such an early hour of the morning, and at the top of his voice—

> With a hey, ho, yeddle;
> And a yeddle, ho, high;
> Coomlachie, Ecclefechan,
> Ardnamurchan and Mulga'ie,
> With a hey, ho, high !

At Sannox, a mile and a half from Corrie, there are two glens coming down to the sea—the South Glen and the North Glen. In going to Loch Ranza you pass the mouth of the first, and turn into the second. The South Glen is the grander of the two. It is a deep and narrow hollow, down into which the great mountains sweep boldly; and, at the end, the flat face of Cior-Mhor forbids egress except by steep and sometimes perilous crag-climbing. It is a place into which one should go alone, and at twilight—if a cloudy twilight, all the better. Then you seem to stand in Nature's workshop, everything you see is vast and awful, the mists

come creeping over Suidhe-Fergus and Cioch-na-h'oighe, shaping themselves to the mountains, but not touching them. Then the night seems to take visible form, and comes down with the clouds into the glen; and, as you stand and listen, there is always a strange sound, made up no doubt of many sounds—the fall of streams, the sough of the wind, the calling of wild birds and of other creatures, but reaching the ear more like a human cry than anything else. The North Glen, through which we go this morning, is of an entirely different character. It is soft, and sometimes melancholy—the South Glen is too stern to be melancholy—the hills on either side are rounded rather than craggy, and there is no precipitous termination, but only a gradual acclivity, over which the road passes at a height of eight or nine hundred feet, and then descends into another glen—that of Chalmadale. In the bright sunlight of to-day, however, and with such a blithe company round us, it is by no means melancholy. Flowers are all about; the speedwell lingering still, the blue harebell swinging on its slender stem, the willow-herb, and the heather—the last, a glorious sight, bursting just now into full bloom and so

W.N. technische Dei

Walker & bottau in Su

Loch Ranza.

beautiful that the heart rises to meet it, as it were, with a fellowship of joy.

We take our long journey leisurely, and by the time we have crossed the summit and begin the descent towards Chalmadale the hot, blue noon is over us. It is really hot—one of the few days of the year of which this could be said, and we make a protracted halt at what is called the Witches' Bridge. I have not been able to find any legend attached to the locality, but I suppose it must be a place where some belated shepherd, hurrying down from the dark moorland, fancied that the witches in pursuit of him were cut off, as in 'Tam o'Shanter,' by the running water. It looks no place for a cold, northern witch or fiend now—rather a haunt for the happy naiad and the gamesome faun.

The stream at this bridge comes down a little scaur in the hillside. The water is clear and sparkling, and the banks are covered with soft cushions of moss and heather; so here we

dispose ourselves in half a dozen groups. One
of our young swains makes music on his pipe ;
my friend John More murmurs appropriate
lines from the Choric song in the ' Lotos Eaters,'
about hearing the downward stream with half-
shut eyes. Then it is proposed that we should
make nonsense-verses, and the Reckless Rhymester, lying on his back and watching the smoke
curl from his cigarette, finishes that amusement
with the following lune:

> Sing you a song of Loch Ranza,
> And knock it all off in a stanza ;
>   There's a castle, the mountains, a bay,
>   And an inn, where they frizzle all day
> Enough for the paunch of a Panza,
>   The herrings they catch in the bay
>   At Loch Ranza.

After this the Moralist threatens to visit the
Rhymester with a 'chunk of old red sandstone';
or, at the least, to lame him with reasons ; and
so we strike our tent and descend for the sea.

At Loch Ranza we lunch and take tea,
always with the accompaniment of herrings,

either eaten or scented on the wind; we watch the Campbelton steamer put off passengers in a tossing cockle-shell of a boat, and, also much to our amusement, tumble empty herring-boxes into the sea, to be picked up at leisure by the fishermen of the village; then some of our young fellows bathe, and while they stand on the shore *in puris naturalibus,* myself and the Critic hold debate as to whether the forked radish looks taller with or without its habilitory environments. Finally, in the cool of the evening, we walk back our eight or nine miles to Corrie, and startle the quiet village with a parting chorus before we turn in for the night.

CHAPTER VII

Suddeine they see from midst of all the Maine
The surging waters like a mountaine rise,
And the great sea, puft up with proud disdaine,
To swell above the measure of his guise,
As threatning to devoure all that his powre despise.
EDMUND SPENSER, *The Faerie Queene.*

CORRIE: *Wednesday, August* 13.

' AFTER our long walk of yesterday, undertaken with cheerfulness and borne with fortitude, may we not indulge ourselves with a sail round the island ? The steamer goes to-morrow.' This was said last night, and we were thinking then of a fair-weather cruise on a summer sea, such as we had once enjoyed before. We imagined ourselves basking on deck in a hot sun, or, if we chose, sheltered under a canvas awning; we saw the hills clear of cloud, or with only a little white mist curling round their summits; the sea was unrippled; globed starfishes in many brilliant colours floated past the ship's side; and when we paused in the bays we could see down and down through the green water thirty, forty feet in depth, to where the great sea-weeds were trailing along the bottom.

The night-watch, however, changed all this, and when the morning broke it seemed removed by a whole season from yesterday. 'How did the change come?' I said to the Provost, who was making his paces as usual along the shore regardless of the weather.

'Oh, at twa o'clock in the mornin', wi' rain an' thunder eneuch to crack the tap o' Goatfell. An' i' the midst o' it a' the lads were haulin' in the herrin's. Indeed, it's a hard life the puir fellows lead.'

'And will the steamer come to-day, Provost?'

The old man, as I have said before, always allows himself a wise latitude in matters connected with meteorological opinion, and so he answered with a long look at the sea, ' Well, she *may* come.' And then, with an equally long look at the sky, ' Or she may no come the day at all. It's no just easy to tell; and there's a deal o' wind outside—a deal o' wind.'

Some of us having made up our minds to go, whatever the weather might be, the usually quiet hours after breakfast were much disturbed by impatient speculations and a continual hurrying to and fro with inquiries about the promised steamer. At length we espied her coming round the corner, beating hard against the wind, and much behind her time. We noticed that she could not come straight into Corrie, as is usual, but that she had to fetch a long sweep round in order to get anywhere near. The faint hearts lingered on the shore, so we gave them a melodramatic good-bye, and put off in the rolling ferry. It was a dangerous little journey, and nearly ended in disaster. There

is always some skill required in bringing the
great steamer and the small boat neatly
together; but on this occasion the difficulty
was much greater than is common. The stalwart boatmen stood up and pulled till the strong
oars were bent like bows, and the muscles
swelled and sloped over their bare brown arms—

> As slopes a wild brook o'er a little stone,
> Running too vehemently to break upon it.

And then, when we got close under the steamer,
it was clear that a mistake had been made. We
were in front of the paddle-box instead of being
behind it. Either the captain of the steamer
had given a wrong order, or the boatmen,
distracted by the tumultuous sea and their own
heavy task, had lost their presence of mind and
thrown up the oars at the wrong time. Whatever the cause, we were in the wrong place. In
an instant we were swept swiftly under the box
and against the wheel. There was a cry of
'Heads down!' and fortunately the order was

F

obeyed.   Had it not been, those who were
nearest the steamer would have had their necks
knocked out, for only by low stooping was there
just room to pass under.   Happily there was no
noise or confusion.   Everybody sat still, seeing
that in that only lay the chance of safety.   Had
there been a rush, with such a sea under us, we
should certainly have gone over, having escaped
one calamity only to fall into another.   It was a
bad five minutes, and many faces though set
firm were very pallid.   Quietly the boat was got
from under the steamer; and, a rope having
been thrown, we were brought-to at the right
point.   Even then it was no easy matter to
land, for the broad-bottomed ferry went up and
down like a feather, and some refused to attempt
it.   The more adventurous spirits sprang up at
the right time, and were then caught by strong
hands and dragged on board.   Some scenes of
rapid movement and short duration, especially
when accompanied with danger, become indelibly

Glen Sannox from the Sea

photographed on the mind. For me this is one of them. I shall always retain a vivid impression of the huge steamer bearing down, as it seemed, mercilessly upon us ; and of the way in which the boatmen looked at each other when it became evident that ' someone had blundered ; ' and of many eyes gazing at us with the anxiety of distress from over the bulwarks of the vessel ; and the expression—that of silent and undemonstrative terror—which settled upon one dear face which was opposite to me in the boat.

The gale was blowing from the south-west, and in passing by the north-east corner of the island and along the Sound of Bute we were surprised to find ourselves in comparatively smooth water and in a warmer air. The circumnavigation of an island either large or small is always a fascinating thing. To-day the clouds were too heavy to permit of our seeing far inland, but the coast was plain enough. The twin glens of Sannox were visible, and in part the

great hills beyond them ; and then came the fine
shore scenery between Sannox and the Cock of
Arran.   The cliffs, or rather the mountain ridge,
is continuous, and rises to about fifteen hundred
feet, being never more than half a mile from the
sea.   We sail near enough to make out the
details and the colour distinctly—the light moss,
the darker green of the grass, the still darker
ferns, the heather, the pink and brown sandstone, and the narrow bright strip of sand.
Beyond this comes Loch Ranza with its Castle,
and its fleet of boats tossing in the harbour.
Then, having rounded the point, we enter the
Sound of Kilbrannan, and begin to feel the force
of the wind which now meets us full in the teeth.
Standing at the prow of the vessel, I realise
what that force is by the way in which it seems
to press on every square inch of exposed flesh,
pushing it back, as it were, from the bone.   We
pitch a good deal now, and the malady of the
sea has already got its victims—they huddle

together in the stern, a melancholy and hopeless crew, provoking in each other that which they would fain avoid; but to those who can stand it the spectacle is fine. A few fishing smacks running with the wind dart past us with amazing celerity, yet there is time to catch the faces of the brave fellows who man them. On the right, across the Sound, is the long low line of Cantire, a deep purple in colour, and strongly contrasting with the greener shores of Arran on our left. And now we pass the lonely but beautiful Bay of Catacol, with Beinn Bhiorach and Beinn Bhreach behind it. Then comes Dugarry and the Duke's Lodge, Mauchrie, and King's Cove. Here, in a cave, The Bruce is said to have sheltered himself in 1307 when he descended on the island for the purpose of seizing Brodick Castle. Those who love the region of dim tradition and thoughts of—

> Old, unhappy, far-off things,
> And battles long ago,

need not rest with a commonplace hero like
Bruce. They may go further back, for here is a
cairn where Columba rested when pursuing his
mission to the heathen inhabitants of Arran ;
and, further still, for here too is the Cave of
Fingal, and the grave of Fingal's daughter.

We get our worst tossing when we come to
round the southern end of the island. We keep
well away from the shore, and are glad when we
have passed the Pladda Lighthouse ; for after
that comes smoother water. They sing a rude
song in the island, part of which I remember,
about the lighthouses in the estuary of the
Clyde, taking them in order, as you go southward, and making the storm culminate appro-
priately at the Pladda :

> As we cam by the Toward Light
>   It blew an unca blast ;
> Says Donald Gray to Duncan More,
>   She'll blow away her mast.
>
> As we cam by the Cumbrae Light
>   It blew an unca gale ;
> Says Donald Gray to Duncan More,
>   We'd best turn round her tail.

As we cam by the Pladda Light
It blew a hurricane;
Says Donald Gray to Duncan More,
I wish we were at hame.

Before we turn northward we get a fine view of Ailsa Craig with its sheer grey cliffs and green sloping summit; and then along the familiar eastern shore of Arran, dropping with passengers into all the bays—Whiting Bay, Lamlash Bay, Brodick Bay, and so round again once more to Corrie.

CHAPTER VIII

' A merry heart is a continual feast.'
   Then take we life and all things in good part :
To fast grows festive while we keep at least
     A merry heart.
   Well pleased with nature and well pleased with art ;
A merry heart makes cheer for man and beast,
   And fancies music in a creaking cart.
Some day, a restful heart whose toils have ceased,
   A heavenly heart gone home from earthly mart :
To-day, blow wind from west or wind from east,
     A merry heart.

           CHRISTINA G. ROSSETTI,
        Songs for Strangers and Pilgrims.

                Thursday, August 14.

'ALL things by turns and nothing long' might be taken for the motto of our weather in Arran just now. Nor would we have it otherwise. Life, movement, variety—that is all we ask. It is monotony that kills. Yesterday, for instance, when we landed in the evening, after our stormy voyage round the island, almost the first thing we saw on shore was a sight eminently suggestive of quietness and peace—

A flock of sheep that leisurely passed by,
One after one.

The wind had dropped, the sky was already clearing, and these sheep were slowly travelling with their shepherd along the road from Brodick. They all moved together, silent and with their heads down—the man as well as the sheep. Coming as we had just done from off the tempestuous fields of ocean, we felt strongly that sentiment which seems so often to have been present to the minds of the ancients, a sentiment arising out of the contrast between the rolling sea with all its dreadful possibilities, and the stable earth which represented to them pastoral occupation, restfulness, safety, and calm.

At half-past eleven the twilight was still

quite brilliant in the north. By that time there
was only one cloud left in the sky; but that one
was immense in size and intensely dark—one
of 'Black Vesper's pageants.' I suppose that
people have always fledged their fancy, as
Antony had done, in speculations as to what the
clouds they see are most like; and as we took
our midnight walk along the beach we talked of
this same cloud. One would have it to be a
nun; but as, clearly enough, it had wings, that
was held to be inadmissible. Another wondered
how we could doubt that it was an eagle—the
eagle of the Caucasus. That was grand enough;
but finally we decided that it should have a
permanent place in our records as the Angel of
Night. Outside this cloud, which filled a third
part of the visible heavens, the stars sparkled as
if there had been frost; and in the south-east
a great planet shone with sufficient strength to
cast a narrow lane of light along the sea just as
the moon does. It was a grand spectacle, and,

as we stood and looked at it, listening at the same time to the steady beat of the tide, we felt ourselves overawed by a sense of fulness and greatness, and by the presence of vast and irresistible forces far off and near, but surrounding us on every side.

We did not need the barometer this morning to tell us how changed the air was, how light and effervescent. To breathe was to live : only to live was to enjoy. Out in the boat, about a hundred yards from the shore, I sat and watched what was going on while the boys pulled slowly to and fro. I cannot hope to set down in words the feeling of the hour. It did not, as last night, consist in a consciousness of vast and oppressive force; but in an impression that some mysterious Spirit of Life was moving in ourselves, and in all the swift and lovely transitions which were momentarily proceeding around us. Behind Am Binnein we saw a thin white cloud rise in the blue and then draw itself, as a

gauzy film, over the purple rocks. In five
minutes there was a refreshing patter of rain
upon our faces; in five minutes more the hot
sun had dried up the moisture. And this was
repeated again and again while we tossed gently
up and down in the boat. Then the clouds all
disappeared, and the day settled into one of
great heat.

In the afternoon I am out in the boat again,
but this time alone. It is too hot to lie on the
rocks, and on the water there is just a faint
breeze. Having pulled myself out of the way of
other craft, I take in the oars and let the boat
move and drift as it will; or, rather, as the
waves will. Leaning idly over the stern what a
fairy region I see under me! I am not far from
the shore, but the water is about twenty feet
deep. Some current carries me gently forward;
and from beneath the boat long streamers of
weed trail for many yards in length. They are
like round cords, brown in colour, but surrounded

by a silvery film which doubles their thickness. When drawn out of the water this film magically disappears, and it is then seen to consist of innumerable minute filaments which are erect in their native element, but which fall when brought into the air.

I note what are the colours of this seascape. The weeds are chiefly brown and yellow, with some little crimson; the water is clear green; the common stones are all gemmed or silvered; and where beds of sand run between them the tint is that of gold. Seen through the medium of the water, the meanest object becomes beautiful. It suffers—

A sea-change
Into something rich and strange.

To utter these words is, of course, to bring before one's mind the whole of that delightful Romance of the Sea which Shakespeare gave us in the calm ending of his days; and no small part of my pleasure, as I lie in the boat, consists in listening with the ear of fancy to those sweet passages in 'The Tempest' which touch upon the subject of the 'salt deep.' Was anyone ever weary of hearing 'Full fathom five,' or 'Come unto these yellow sands'? Surely these are among those

Sounds and sweet airs, that give delight and hurt not.

While these enchanted measures are running through my mind I discover that I have drifted too near the shore. A friend shouts to me from the road under the cliffs, and I hear the keel grating on the stones. My dream is over and I pull out to sea again; but not without noticing how curiously, as I go into deeper water, the sea-bottom appears to sink or recede from under me, so that I feel as if I were falling into an ever-deepening gulf from which all objects that measure distance gradually disappear. Under certain aspects the bottom of the sea suggests to the mind only images of undisguised horror. There is, however, another aspect—that which I have just seen—which presents a more than earthly beauty, and of which we find traces in the romantic legends of all countries.

When I have got away from the shore I find another wonderful sight waiting for me. The sun, though falling westward, is yet high in the heavens; and the great mountains present an appearance not very often observed, and to me more awful than any other. They stand in their own shadows; they are dark from excess of light; and, though perfectly clear, their altitude is exaggerated as if by mist. The effect is increased by the fact that down into some of the hollows a ray of light streams, cutting the shadow sharply as with a knife.

The hot afternoon tempted our young people to hold a 'gipsy tea' on the shore at North Sannox. A gipsy tea is an institution in which I have lost faith; unless it is to be celebrated on some breezy upland, where the midges dare not come. On the shore, at any rate, the experiment is a snare and a delusion. Creeping things innumerable get in among all the eatables; and marvellous flying creatures per-

North Sannox Shore

vade all the drinkables; and so I kept away, spending my time instead on the water; but in the evening I went to fetch the company home. They looked rather doleful, and had got their arms and faces much bitten; but these inconveniences were soon forgotten in the pleasure of a memorable evening walk. The sea was now light blue, and so calm that it reflected like a lake the white clouds that were over it, and the boats with their masts and sails as they lay upon its surface. As we come up from the shore and traverse the heathery moorland we find that the sunset has gone; but the clear twilight remains; and, as we look at the mountains beyond the moor, some of us are constrained to linger in silence—held back by the fascination of a scene so still, so solemn, that in the midst of it even to speak aloud seems to be a desecration, until at length one whispers to me words which recall that strange episode on the Mount of Transfiguration—words which were already in my own mind— 'Master, it is good for us to be here.'

G

CHAPTER IX

Deep peace abides within the glen profound,
 Though gaunt the heights its purple depth that rim—
 Peaks of the Castles and the visage grim
Of dark Cir Mhor : no sound, nor ghost of sound
Comes to me here ; only, where rowans bound
 The crystal burn, it croons its evening hymn,
 And the wind stirs the reeds ; while vast and dim,
Dimmer and vaster grow the hills around.

The home of solitude indeed is thine,
 Sannox !   Man turns from thee, he dare not stay
'Neath those eternal peaks in jaggèd line
 That scorn his puny frame and little day :
He seeks the sea-marge where white houses shine,
 And boats are moor'd within the sheltering bay.
      Cuthbert E. Tyrer, *Glen Sannox, Arran.*

     Corrie : *Friday, August* 15.

My journal broke off yesterday with the twilight
on the moor. The day had been, in our sense
of the word, an eventful one, eventful to those

who care for *nature-study*, those by whom all the phenomena of the world, whether great or small, are regarded with interest no less for their beauty than for the suggestive intelligence which is felt to be moving behind them.

We lingered for a long time on the moor-land. We know what a charm there is in sitting, very quiet and still, within some chamber already almost dark, watching the clear light of evening fade out of the sky. It was the same on the moor. The night seemed already to have reached the undulating circle of rock and heather in midst of which we stood; but the mountains, towards whose summits our eyes were lifted, seemed as if they might stand for ever unchanging in the radiance, clear if not brilliant, which still filled the west.

The day had been, as we have said, an eventful one; and yet the story of it was not finished. The way from the moor, passing close by the kirk and the manse, dips into a

narrow and sandy lane. Here horses and
vehicles ford the river; but foot passengers
turn aside and cross by a little wooden bridge.
At this point we come upon a sedate and yet
happy company of peasants and fisher-folk
from the village. Their demeanour is in accord
with the landscape. We pause and talk with
them. They have been to some little week-
night meeting for devotion held at the manse,
and the young man who is their pastor is
setting them forward on their way home. It
is pleasant to listen to their talk—gossip without garrulousness or levity, the quiet and simple interchange of news about what interests
them in the cottage and on the sea. Most of
them are elderly women, but there are also
some men and boys. Among them is poor
Janet M'Bride. She is lame; but they walk
slowly enough even for her. Janet is a 'lone
woman'—she has neither chick nor child, and
lives in a queer little cabin of wood in which

there is only just room for a fire and a couch.
She came to the island as a servant when she
was but a girl, and has lived on it ever since,
and they will not send her away.   She spins
wool on an old wheel and knits a few stockings ;

JANET M'BRIDE.

but her fingers are stiff with rheumatism, and
if those who are themselves poor enough were
not kind to her it would go ill with Janet in
the winter-time.   When we reached the lane
which turns from the high road by the sea and

runs up into South Sannox Glen, we bade good-night to Janet and her friends. Their faces showed how happy they were, and I said to my companion, 'Who would rob them of that which not only breaks the monotony of their existence, but which also brings to them consolation of the highest kind?'

We had observed as we passed that the long twilight was still in the glen, and, although it was growing late, we could not refuse the opportunity offered of seeing the familiar scene under conditions which might not recur. We pushed on as far as the base of Cioch-na-h'oighe —it was not safe to go further. Then we stood and listened to the river roaring in unseen depths, and watched with amazement the great wall of mountains in front of us, dark yet clear, so clear that every fantastic peak and each serrated edge was drawn in strong and un- graduated outline across the plane of the sky. As we returned we saw a light appear on the crest of a low hill towards the east. It was so large and brilliant that we were all mistaken as to its nature. We said, 'Some shepherd is abroad with his lantern, folding the flocks or seeking for strayed sheep.' But when we looked again we saw it was the evening star, preternaturally large, and climbing above the ridge. As we go forward it disappears; but by stepping slowly back we reproduce the aspect of its rising. On the road by the shore there is a stillness such as we have not experienced before. There is no wind. The wood on our right is silent; not a leaf rustles; no bird moves; even the wild pigeons are at rest. The sea on our left is silent also. Though we stand and listen intently we cannot hear a wave break on the shore. At last, when our ears are stretched to the utmost, a fish leaps, and is heard falling back into the water. As we get nearer the village, sounds begin to reach us, and the first is the voice of a boy, who, as he comes out of the dark, sings with unaffected simplicity a few bars of 'Home, sweet home.' We know the lad, and give him a cheery good-night. He has far to go and along a lonely road, for his home is at the shepherd's farm on the hill side, beyond North Sannox. He will have to skirt the shore, then past the kirk and across the moorland, where the track is dim and uncertain; but worse than that, he must cross two burns thickly embowered with wood, where superstitious fears may well make him tremble. 'Keep a brave heart, my little man, and a sure foot, for the stepping-stones are wide apart and the water runs deep in the second burn.'

To-day we have great heat and hardly any wind. The sea is purple in colour and shore-less, for hot-looking clouds hide all the land north and east. In the afternoon we take the steamer to Brodick and venture to explore Glen

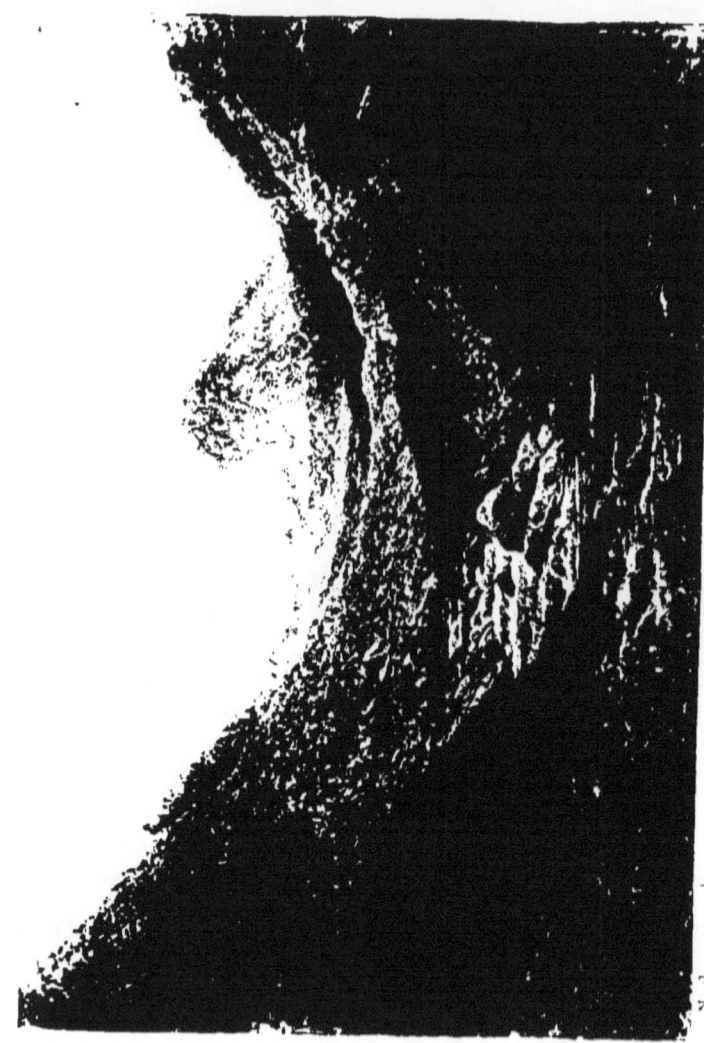

Walker & Boutall Ph Sc

N.1 [unclear] 1 1

Glen Rosa.

Rosa. It is not a well-chosen day. The heat is too great, the hills look low and their hue is monotonous. We rest a long time by the Shirag Burn, in a cool nook under the bridge, where we can see the brown trout darting among the stones. Then, the heat having abated a little, we press forward by the mouth of Glen Shirag, from which, looking east, there is a fine view of the wide plain, covered with grass and corn, and beyond that, the park, and Brodick Castle, and the sea. From Shirag we come to Glen Shant, where the principal feature is the broad river flowing over white pebbles, and the great precipice of slate which rises above it to the height of eleven hundred feet. Passing through Glen Shant, the entrance to Glen Rosa is marked by the wild torrent—the Garbh-Alt—which comes dashing down from Ben-Ghnuis, and leaps at last into the Rosa Burn, where it runs quietly between walls of gray rock. Here my young companions turn back, for the path becomes bad, and they are very weary; but I continue the walk. On the right is the shoulder of Goatfell; on the left Ben-Cliabhain; and in front Cior-Mhor and the Col, which separates Glen Rosa from Glen Sannox.

The Rosa Glen is a fine piece of scenery, no doubt, but it is not equal to its rival at Sannox. It is larger, but it is neither so wild nor so grandly symmetrical in the lines of its composition. It is always a surprise when one hears for the first time that the *col* or saddle is all that separates the two glens. Both start from the sea; but, instead of running directly inland, they sweep round, and would join each other if it were not for the apparently inaccessible rampart of rock which divides them, by crossing from the base of Goatfell to that of Cior-Mhor. It is said that the practicability of passing from Rosa into Sannox was not known until recent years, except by a few shepherds who had occasionally tried it.

When I get near to the foot of this barrier I
see coming down towards me, out of the clouds,
with break-neck strides, two stalwart athletes
whom I know. They have come from Corrie,
and are making the circuit of the two glens.
As it is hardly likely that I should get well over
before dusk, I decide to return with them along
Glen Rosa. We sit down for a few minutes on
a dry patch of heather—not easy to find—while
they smoke their pipes, and then we start homeward at a great pace, with trousers turned up
and shirts turned back, careless of the way,
leaping from rock to rock, and out of one spongy
hole into another. I admire their agility, and
follow as well as I may. It is a good six miles
back through the glen, and six miles more along
the high-road by the sea. By the time we reach
Corrie, I have had quite enough of it; but after
a smart rubbing down, I am ready for the
evening meal, and not indisposed for the well-
earned rest which is to follow.

CHAPTER X

Sport that wrinkled care derides,
And laughter holding both his sides.

> MILTON, *L'Allegro.*

By sports like these are all their cares beguiled;
The sports of children satisfy the child.

> GOLDSMITH, *The Traveller.*

CORRIE : *Saturday, August* 16.

WIND north-east. It is curious that with the wind in this quarter we always have the sea muddy, and yellow in colour. As I go down to take my bath, in the usual costume—that of an Arabian sheikh—I meet the boys running back; they look like small Arabian sheikhs. They dare not bathe, they say; the creek is full of jelly-fish. This is another unfailing result of a north-east wind. I drag the young rascals back ; but nothing will induce them to enter the water. As they stand at the edge, they perform a dance of agony and point to the abhorred *Medusæ* gyrating in the tide. To show my bravery I plunge in myself; but the dip is no luxury, for I have to keep my eye on the uncanny creatures as they float round me ; and, sometimes, to kick them with my feet. Later in the morning a young fellow gets badly stung, and all sorts of remedies are tried ; but it takes hours to bring him round. Having been once stung myself, I know the sensation and remember it acutely, though it is more than thirty years ago. I shudder as I recall the grasp of the antennæ ; the instantaneous injection of the poison ; the slimy touch as I caught the creature in my hand and flung it over the sea ; and then the rubbing of my skin with dry salt, and the incessant pacing up and down my chamber for seven long hours. Only in that way could the virus be got rid of. In my case to sit down even for a moment was to sleep, and then to fall into great torture.

About noon the wind changes, and the sea clears rapidly, becoming its own bright blue again. On the shore I meet the Provost. ' Well, Provost, how about the jelly-fish ? What brings them here—is it the wind ? ' The Provost would sooner perish than fail to give a reason when challenged. The mysteries of nature and of theology are all open to him, and he answers without hesitation, ' It's nae the wind at a'—it's this ' (in a low whisper) : ' August is just the breeding month for a' craytures on land and sea. The air's full o' strange flies and the water's swarming wi' queer things, the like o' which ye'll never see at any ither time ; an' that's the reason o' it.' If the Provost had solved the riddle of the Sphinx, he could not have given a prouder toss to his white head or looked with more pity upon the ignorant Southron who was standing by his side.

In the evening the wonted quiet of the village is invaded by strange sights and sounds. We have become suddenly and exuberantly festive. Happily there is neither bill-poster nor bellman in Corrie; but a curious little placard, fastened with some ingenuity to the face of a rock, has made us aware during the last few days that at the end of the week we might expect the Annual Sports. And here we are in the midst of them. There are races by land and by sea. The latter are intensely exciting. The boatmen are all known to us, and each has his favourite. If the fate of an empire hung upon the stroke we could not be more demonstrative in our enthusiasm, and the wonder is that one-half of us do not push the other half into the water. We get the most amusement, however, out of what is called the 'Greased Jibboom.' A boat is taken a little way from the shore. The mast of a lugger is lashed to the stem so as to stretch over the water like a jib. A man goes out in a smaller boat and covers the mast with grease; then he hangs a leg of mutton at the extremity. When all is ready the competitors, partially clothed, begin the contest. They have to walk the long greased pole with bare feet, and snatch away the mutton as they fall into the water. Nine times out of ten a man will fall long before he comes near the point. He takes a step or two forward, then there comes a wave, the boat sways, the mast goes up and down, the slippery foothold is lost, you see a figure ludicrously quivering in the air, and then down he goes, head over heels, in the water; he swims round, and while he is being pulled into the boat another competitor tries his fortune. The interest is increased by the fact that a number of young exquisites—visitors from the hotel— have entered the lists against the boatmen. They have no chance, however, and as one 'curled darling' after another tumbles ignominiously into the water, the ladies on the shore clap their hands and scream with delight When Tom M'Murdo at last wins the prize, he swims to the beach, holding the mutton aloft in one hand. Corrie rings with plaudits; and it is a pretty sight to see Tom's wife take the mutton from her dripping husband, and, after wiping the salt water from it with her apron, bear it away to the cottage on the hillside. The 'weans' will have an unusual feast to-morrow.

After dark there are fireworks—coloured lights on the beach, and audacious rockets which pretend that they are going up among the stars, and then come down precipitately and extinguish themselves with a fizz in the water. But, best of all, we thought, were the torches carried rapidly up and down among the trees in the upland garden, behind the inn, and casting the most fantastic and inexplicable shadows across the road and on to the sea. It is all very grand, and the young folks have

H

relished it immensely; but now, at midnight, I am thankful it is over. The noise and the shouting have ceased; the roisterers have all gone, some to a yacht which lies off the shore; some to Brodick, some to Loch Ranza—the last will have a wild and lonely ride through the moonless night—and Corrie is once more restored to its native quiet. As I walk up and down before the door of our house I hear nothing but the wind on the mountain, and the gurgle of the tide as it rushes up the estuary.

Monday, August 18.

Beginning in the early morning, the rain lasted yesterday until evening. The landscape was grey and cool; the sea, a slate-coloured green, passing at the horizon into a line of black. At eight o'clock, when the rain ceased, although the sky did not clear, we could not help noting what a soft light fell upon all things—more beautiful than that of many a brilliant sunset—and how perfect was the harmony of sea and shore and village.

This morning the weather was fine again. In the garden behind the house a pair of blackbirds were feeding fearlessly on the currants, which had been left hanging too long on the bushes. They seemed to say, 'What you are foolish enough to neglect, surely we may gather without molestation.' It is pleasant to take a few paces in this garden after breakfast. At the upper end, where a tall hedge separates it from the brae-side, the creamy flowers are thick on the privet; in one corner a fuchsia hangs heavy with bloom, and above it the honeysuckle climbs up and clings to the branches of a birch.

In the afternoon I am out in the boat. There is no wind; and yet there is a great heaving on the sea—which I much enjoy—a grand roll, 'mighty mouthed,' like the movement of an epic line. The motive of it is somewhere far away, out of our ken, where storms have been raging, though here we have had nothing but calm. Later on we wander, as usual, along the beach northward. A misty and yellow evening light falls on the low hills at North Sannox. Its influence lowers and subdues them, and their tone is, as usual, not without a touch of melancholy. The lofty peaks at South Sannox, on the contrary, stand, 'commercing with the skies,' in a clear light, which seems to give them *elevation*, not in altitude only, but in feeling. So true is it, 'To that which hath shall be given; and from that which hath not, shall be taken away even that which it hath.'

CHAPTER XI

Not more serenely 'neath the southern pine
  White glistening beaches meet blue ocean's kiss :
  No soft Italian strand more fair than this,—
Not Shelley's Spezzia, nor the shore divine
Where Virgil sleeps in cypress-darkened shrine.
  Here nought should fall unseemly or amiss ;
  Lulled by these woods and waters, life were bliss,
Though touch'd with shade from yon dark mountain-line.

And oh, dear burn ! most exquisite of brooks !
  The rowan loves thee, and the birch-clad braes
    Cast beryl shadows on thy crystal flow.
  None of the famous streams that poets praise
  Have lovelier pools, that charm the gazer's looks
    As though a fabled Naiad slept below.

CUTHBERT E. TYRER, *Sannox Shore.*

CORRIE : *Tuesday, August* 19.

ALTHOUGH, for a lodging, we prefer the snug
cheerfulness of Corrie, it is to Sannox, a mile
and a half away, that we go most frequently for

delectation. There the two streams come down
the two diverse glens and fall into the sea.
The mouths of the two rivers are not quite a
mile asunder; nor has either of them an ex-
tensive course; yet nowhere else in Arran can
you get such variety, or find such noble pictures
as are to be seen on the banks of these streams
and in the bit of country which lies between
them. Both burns rise in the heart of the
hills, and amid scenes of the grandest character;
but their immediate banks are not remarkable
until they are about half a mile from the sea;
then, the South Burn entering a rocky glen
and the North Burn hiding itself in a dense
wood, they become interesting in the highest
degree. From a ridge under the loftier hills, at
a place called Mid Sannox, which is between
the two streams, there is one of the most
perfect views in the Island. Looking inland
you get the whole of the South Glen; and,
beyond it, the wild peaks in Glen Rosa. A

turn of the head, and you are able to follow the North Glen as far as the first bridge on the Loch Ranza road. Then, looking seaward, the Estuary of the Clyde takes the appearance of a great lake; and, when the skies are clear and the water blue, there is much, both in the contour of the shore and the appearance of the sea, which suggests the idea of Italian beauty. Let me add another word: choose a stormy day for a view up the Glens, and a still one for that across the sea.

We were talking these things over as we lingered about Sannox last night. Coming along the lane out of the South Glen and past the old graveyard of Saint Michael, we were overtaken by a homeward-bound bee which was hurrying down from its heather-pasturage on the heights. It swept past us with a loud hum which sounded like a note of pride and satisfaction. There is fine feeding here for bees; and loads of hives are brought over on the

steamers from the mainland and carried up on
to the mountains to be left there for the season.
This lane has a character of its own, and one
that suits the lonely burial-place beside it.   It
is broken and straggling.   Along each side you
will find the hemlock, the thistle, and the sorrel.
When night approaches the bats are always
overhead and usually an obese and unctuous-
looking toad will be seen creeping across the
path.   All these things are connected with a
feeling of desolation ; but even here the tenderness and beauty of nature find expression in
the delicate harebell which waves its blossom
under the taller and coarser herbage.

At the bottom of the lane, where you come
upon the shore, there is a patch of common
where the bracken and the furze grow on the
turf.   Beyond this the South Burn, winding
down to the sea and turning acutely so as to
come at right angles with the shore, has thrown
up a bank of sand on which there has rested

for many long years a black dismantled hull. Through its shrunken ribs the sky may be seen, and one thinks of the hardy fellows who once guided its keel along the deep, and who now slumber in the mountain graveyard which we

have just passed. The river bed is very shallow, but when a flood-tide has been flowing we have once or twice navigated our boat from the sea and up the stream till we have found ourselves under the green birch boughs just below the footbridge.

When we got back to the village the daylight was gone; but on the harbour-bridge a
little pastoral was being enacted which made us
pause.   The bridge is the nucleus of Corrie.
It was here, no doubt, that the hamlet had its
beginning.   At this point the sea had beaten in
so close to the hill-foot that there was not room
for the road to pass.   The head of the narrow
gulley has, therefore, been bridged over.   No
stream flows under, and there is a parapet only
on the side next the sea.   Here, with unhewn
stones, a rude harbour has been constructed in
which there is space enough for three or four
fishing smacks to lie, so that when you stand
on the bridge—which, after all, is only half a
bridge—you look down on one hand to the
water, while on the other you look up a dry
ravine.   On one side of this, and close by, are
some limestone caves.   These are not worked
now, and in the largest of them the blacksmith
of the village plies his trade.   The limestone

accounts, at once, both for Corrie and its little harbour, and, as I have said, from this point the village has naturally extended itself. In the daytime the gathering ground is a few yards further south, at the creek, off which the steamers now stop; but at night, probably from the force of habit, the native population always repairs to the harbour.

As we approached this place last night, on our way home from Sannox, we heard music and laughter. On the low parapet of the bridge was seated a man with an accordion. He played the simple instrument with some skill, waving it about in his hands and following his own notes by beating on the ground with his foot. In front of him were about a score of dancers. The couples were made up of the rough fisher-lads and strapping lassies of the village; yet, though there was plenty of vigour, there was neither rudeness nor vulgarity. Indeed, some of them displayed an unaffected

grace combined with hearty enjoyment which
would have put to shame much of the insipid
posturing which often passes for dancing in
politer circles.

The dance was, of course, the Scottish reel.
It seemed to have no end, and as I watched it
going on and on with ever increasing demon-
strativeness, it was as much as I could do to
keep myself from dashing into the vortex. I
compromised the matter, however, by humming
to myself certain well-known hexameters in
' The Bothie of Tober-na-Vuolich,' which imi-
tate admirably the steps of the reel :—

Lo ! I see piping and dancing! and whom in the midst of
    the battle
Cantering loudly along there, or, look you with arms uplifted,
Whistling, and snapping his fingers, and seizing his gay
    smiling Janet,
Whom? whom else but the Piper? the wary precognisant
    Piper ;—
So with the music possessing him, swaying him, goeth he,
    look you,
Swinging and flinging, and stamping and tramping, and
    grasping and clasping
Whom but gay Janet?

It was indeed a pleasant picture with the starlight overhead, and around us for background the shadowy mountain side, and the cottages with their open doors; and, towards the sea, the tall ships' masts swaying to and fro as the tide began to flow into the harbour. 'Is it not a pity,' we said, as we turned to go, ' that there should be left for our people so little of healthy outdoor enjoyment such as we have seen here to-night?' On inquiry we found that these dances were regularly held whenever the musician could be got.

And the musician: what of him? He deserves a passing word, for like the dance he seems to belong to an Arcadian period which has almost entirely disappeared. He is a packman who walks round the island about once a month. He carries a heavy burden on his back and, having his hands at liberty, he plays his simple music for his own pleasure as he trudges along. I have often met him playing on lonely

roads when there was none to hear. Whenever
he is at Corrie his services are at the disposal
of the villagers, and he will take no money for
hire. His face is grave yet cheerful; and his
garb is that of a man in a much higher station
of life. It is impossible to see him without
thinking of two figures in our literature:
Goldsmith's own sketch of himself—

> How often have I led thy sportive choir,
> With tuneless pipe, beside the murmuring Loire?
> And haply, though my harsh touch, faltering still,
> But mocked all tune, and marr'd the dancer's skill,
> Yet would the village praise my wondrous power,
> And dance, forgetful of the noontide hour.

And Wordsworth's picture of the Pedlar in the
'Excursion'—

> A vagrant Merchant under a heavy load
> Bent as he moves, and needing frequent rest:
> Yet do such travellers find their own delight;
> And their hard service, deemed debasing now,
> Gained merited respect in simpler times;
> When squire and priest, and they who round them dwelt
> In rustic sequestration—all dependent
> Upon the Pedlar's toil—supplied their wants,
> Or pleased their fancies with the wares he brought.

CHAPTER XII

The ocean with its vastness, its blue green,
  Its ships, its rocks, its caves, its hopes, its fears,--
  Its voice mysterious, which whoso hears
Must think on what will be, and what has been.

JOHN KEATS, To my Brother George.

CORRIE : Friday, August 22.

A CONSIDERABLE part of the last few days has been spent alone and on the water. And here is the Log. The voyage was from the Clyde to the Mersey, and back again. At three o'clock in the afternoon we leave Corrie by a returning steamer, and make straight for Garroch Head, the southern promontory of Bute. We keep our faces turned towards that white house on the shore which has now acquired for us something of the sacredness of home. The air is clear, and for miles we can distinguish the handkerchiefs which are being waved in token of protracted farewell. It is curious to note how, as we recede, the Island seems to rise upon us, the rapid motion of the vessel communicating itself to the land. First the belt of rocky wood and of houses ; then the high green shelf which means the old sea-level; and last the great serrated peaks which start up from behind and even seem to curve over towards the sea. When we have almost reached Bute, which is twelve miles from Arran, we, who know it so well, can still make out the white house on the shore, and discriminate it from the other grey dots by which it is surrounded.

The steamer runs close to Garroch Head. A dry and desolate hollow slopes down to the sea. ' Nant Vortigern on a smaller scale,' we say. In the midst is a fire, smoking, but with no one near to tend it. It is a gipsy fire probably, and we observe that it heightens the effect of loneliness.

Running west of the two Cumbraes, and under Largs, where Haco the Norwegian lost his battle against the Scotch seven hundred years ago, we come into the Frith of Clyde. Twenty miles further and we are in that fine centre where the Estuary, the Holy Loch, Loch Long, the Gareloch, and the real mouth of the Clyde, like five great water-ways, converge and meet as in a vast basin.

We are no sooner in the Clyde itself than the scene changes. We are environed by a low-hung-cloud of fog and smoke. The sun shines over it and on to it, and even casts a gleam on the water near us; but the wall of mist is impenetrable to the eye, and phantom ships, enormously heightened in size, sail in and out of it with strange effect. We only say one word, and that is enough—'Turner.'

And now, unfortunately, we must linger at

I

Greenock till eight o'clock.   It is a weary place ;
dismal and dreary beyond description. We cannot bear to walk about its streets.   The trees
are stunted, the houses are squalid, and the
churches !—over them we draw a veil, and pray
that the mind may charitably forget them.

The rattling of the steam-winch, hauling
cargo on the larger boat to which we have been
transferred, is a terrible trial for the nerves ;
but even that is not so bad as the ghastly
grimness of Greenock and its churches, loom-
ing upon us through the misty autumn twilight.

Back now along the Estuary of the Clyde as
night falls on the sea.   At Millport the lights
are twinkling in the harbour.   It is quite dark
by the time we are off Arran ; so dark that I
am not able to say whether the familiar mountain outlines are really discerned by the natural
eye, or only, with the aid of memory, sketched
by the imagination.   It is quite certain, however,
that the white house on the shore is altogether

beyond our sight; yet we dissemble with ourselves, and feign that we recognise its locality.

What brilliant green star is that on our right? We are told it is the lighthouse on Holy Island, off Lamlash. Then we catch the Pladda Light, and part company with an Irish steamer which, turning suddenly west, makes for the Mull of Cantire and the North Channel. How strange it looks, passing away into the vacancy of night, its red cabin-lights apparently burning close to the water!

About midnight we pass Ailsa Craig on the east. A seaman tells us it is two miles away. A more extraordinary apparition I have never seen. We have no moon nor any stars; and in the dim light the great rock is neither what Keats called it in prose—'A transparent tortoise asleep upon the calm water;' nor what he named it in his imperishable verse—a 'craggy ocean-pyramid'—but something wilder than these; a vast shapeless Incubus; black and awful ; hanging in the sky, or brooding over the water. It seems to be so clearly detached from the sea that we need to be told again and again that it is really Ailsa at which we are gazing. The truth is, I suppose, that the dark plain of the sea is not distinguishable from the equally dark arch of the sky.

Six o'clock in the morning : and I am taking my first turn upon deck. We are passing the Isle of Man. How cold it looks—how grey and misty and cheerless ! We are near enough to see the waves flinging themselves on the rocks, and falling hopelessly back again into the gulf from which they hoped to rise. Item : Sleep no more in these cabin berths. The stifling atmosphere brings nightmare. Once I had the whole incumbency of Ailsa upon me. When I woke and looked round, my fellow sleepers seemed for all the world like dead men on the shelves of a mausoleum. When one of them lifts up his head with a mechanical motion, like that of a piece of waxwork, glares at me, and then drops back again, the horror of the situation is increased. Just before daylight a dark-looking creature—gnome, familiar spirit, or demon—comes in, and after creeping stealthily round—I wonder apprehensively what it is that he would be at—blows out the oil lamp which swings in the centre. After this the smell is intolerable; and, rolling my grave-clothes in a heap, and taking all my earthly habiliments in my hands, I clear away and dress outside on the cabin stairs. It is a happy deliverance! Nature's second course has been no nourisher to me. But now the fresh breeze on deck does what sleep has left undone, and as we speed along the morning brightens.

Yonder is the Welsh coast, clearly seen, from Penmaenmawr to the wide mouth of the Dee.

About noon we pass out of sunlight into smoke, and know that we are close upon Liverpool.

At two o'clock of the next day we start upon
the return voyage.   At seven in the evening we
again sight the Isle of Man; and note, as we
draw near to it, the gradual development of
colour and of marking in the green fields and on
the rocky shore.   We pass so close that even in
the twilight we can see people walking on the
beach, and a man dragging a boat to the top
of the shingle.

As we pass the Point of Ayre, the northern
extremity of the Isle of Man, the lamp in the
lighthouse is being lit, and the beams flash
across the darkening water.   At the same time
the ship's lights are hauled up, and I hear the
cry, ' The look-out is set, sir.'   That means that
I must give up my ' coign of vantage ' on the
forecastle deck to an old seaman who will watch
there alone, and undisturbed.   It is a fine thing
to observe the descent of night on the open sea.
The sun has gone, and the sky is partially
clouded, but from open spaces a light still falls.

I have arranged with the steward to make up my berth on deck, under the covered passage at the head of the cabin stairs. And now that the last of the passengers has disappeared I am alone with the captain, the ' look-out,' and the man in the wheel-house. Leaning over the bulwark, I watch the wavering horizon and listen to the sound, like thunder, which the vessel makes in cleaving the water. There is no other noise except that of the wind, which has now risen to a gale. Sometimes there is a dash of rain, and then it becomes suddenly clear and starry. When we pass the Portpatrick Light, which is off Stranraer and opposite Belfast Lough, it is between twelve and one, and I think it time to turn in.

Out again at four o'clock in the morning. The stars are still bright; but the dawn is breaking. Large confused clouds almost cover the sky; but behind them we see that the sky is clear. Then, though the sun is invisible, the heavens are flushed with crimson just as we come in front of Arran.

And now we strain our eyes to catch, if we may, the white house on the shore. It is impossible; but what matter, the heart reaches it, if the eye cannot; and I croon over to myself those delightful lines with which dear old Titmarsh concludes his poem of ' The White Squall '—

And as the sunrise splendid
    Came blushing o'er the sea,
I thought as day was breaking,
My little girls were waking,
And smiling, and making
    A prayer at home for me.

W.B. dith J.H. Del.   Walker & Boutall Ph. Sc.

"Corrie from the landing rock."

CHAPTER XIII

When summer's faltering hand
Yields her capricious sceptre to the grasp
Of noble autumn, days will intervene
Of an elysian softness which belongs
To other lands, not by our seasons claimed.

F. W. FABER. *Sir Lancelot.*

CORRIE : *Sunday, August* 24.

THIS is the most perfect day of the whole month.
The wind is in the south-east. The air is soft
and warm, yet clear. It is now, in the early
afternoon, high-tide—high and full. The sea,
although not rough, is instinct with changeful
life and joyous motion. The islands and the far
shores are so distinct that we can make out the
crescent houses and the Cathedral spire on the
Greater Cumbrae, and even the turn and the
colour of Fairlie Glen on the mainland twenty
miles away. The water in the distance wears a

deep purple; nearer the land it is blue; inshore it is green. The young folks are sitting on the rocks in the open sunshine; we elders are out of doors also, but in the protecting shadow of the house. On the earth, on the sea, in the sky there is no jarring note; and it would be shame to us if we ourselves were out of tune. One who sits beside me on the bench recalls to my mind a passage—a favourite one with both of us—which is appropriate to the occasion and the hour. It will be found in that brief memoir of Keats prefixed by Lord Houghton to the edition of the Poems published in 1854. It has some-how slipped out of the later and more complete ' Life and Letters ' by the same writer. The Mr. Bailey alluded to was an early acquaintance of the poet's who afterwards became Archdeacon of Colombo, in Ceylon. ' In September, Keats visited his friend Bailey, at Oxford, and wrote thence as follows :—" Believe me, my dear ——, it is a great happiness to me that you are, in the

finest part of the year, winning a little enjoyment from the hard world. In truth, the great
Elements we know of are no mean comforters :
the open sky sits upon our senses like a sapphire
crown ; the air is our robe of state ; the earth
is our throne ; and the sea a mighty minstrel
playing before it—able, like David's harp, to
make such a one as you forget almost the tempest
cares of life." '

This undisturbed beauty, this sweet peaceful-
ness, as of a Sabbath beyond that which comes
with the mere procession of time, are the more
acceptable because both yesterday and Friday
were wild and stormy. The last leaf of this
Journal closed as we sighted Arran from the
deck of the steamer, with the sky reddening for
sunrise. If we could have left that steamer
there and then, and made straight for Corrie we
should, although the sea was rough, have been
delighted to do it. We might then have had our
morning dip, and joined the circle at breakfast.

We must needs go on, however, and the worst was we knew that it must end in another detention at that baleful Greenock. As we passed the lighthouse on what the Scotch call the Wee Cumrae, we saw the lamp extinguished; just as, when the night was beginning, we had seen it kindled at the Point of Ayre. I can hardly tell why, but these lighthouses have for me a great fascination. I cannot help regarding them as substantial entities, which stand like sentinels, and do their duty bravely, having within them a spirit of life which the lamp symbolises.

It was too true. We reached Greenock at five o'clock, and were told we must wait there until about ten, at which time the *Guinevere* would take us back to Arran. The passengers, looking very mournful, came up one by one out of their berths and would talk to us on deck. The rattling of the steam-winch had roused them. What strange creatures we meet on such a voyage! One of these had come to see Scotland, but he had no idea where he must go or what it was that he would see. He had been told that this was a Scotch steamer, and he thought it would be all right. Poor fellow! he might well look appalled when he found himself

in Greenock. Another told me he thought all the islands in the Clyde were sterile and un-inhabited. And a third, whom I had not seen before, came and whispered to me—'I see the King of Spain is going to marry again.' I looked hard at him, but there was no lunacy in his eye, and I answered, 'What's Hecuba to me or I to Hecuba?' After that there were evidently doubts on his mind as to *my* sanity.

About eight o'clock we found a means of escape. The *Lord of the Isles* was starting on her daily trip to Inverary. We could travel by her as far as Dunoon and wait there for the *Guinevere*; and besides, we could breakfast as we journeyed. The *Lord of the Isles* is a magnificently appointed boat, and her meals are admirable. I know a shrewd old Scotchman whose best ideal of pleasure is to travel by this boat or the *Iona*, backwards and forwards, day after day. He says: 'You get pure air; the most splendid scenery in the kingdom; music, society, and excellent feeding at less than hotel prices;' and besides, he adds, 'you can have your boots cleaned on board; and buy your penny paper, or your pound of apples; and the whisky—well, that's just fine.'

We had an hour or two in Dunoon, a beautiful place enough for those who do not care for seclusion, and then, having joined the *Guinevere*, we ran into Corrie with a tearing wind behind us.

Towards nightfall we ventured out in our own little boat; but were glad to hurry back. Both land and sea had a strangely threatening aspect. The sky was covered with horizontal masses of cloud, which gave to everything beneath them an unearthly colour—that blue, or purple, which is almost black. As we pulled hard into the creek, the high summit of Am-Binnein seemed so near that it might have been taken for a rock overhanging the fields.

The night which followed was, of course, wet and stormy. Not a glimmer of light could be discovered; and the blind sea roared through the dark like a Titan in pain, and dashed itself on the ledges with a sound as of thunder.

How strangely such a scene as this contrasts
with that upon which, in the same place, we are
now gazing!   And what must it be in the
winter! The good wife of the house here tells
us, with graphic touches of her own, and not
without some pride in her achievement, how one
Christmas night when a gale was raging from
the east and the air was thick with falling flakes
of snow, she heard, sitting late by the fire, the
fog-horn sounding in the channel.   She listened.
It came nearer.   Again, nearer, and nearer
still.   Once more, so near that it seemed as if it
had been blown upon the beach below.   Then
she sprang to her feet, and called to her father,
who was asleep, ' John Campbell, there is a ship
drifting on the rocks, God help us ! '   Quickly
she lighted the old lantern, and, throwing a
blanket over her shoulders, she rushed out into
the storm.   There was not a moment to lose;
and, at the peril of her own life, she ran along
the narrow and slippery ledge of rock which

leads to the outermost point. One false step and she would have fallen where the receding wave would have dragged her beyond hope of retrieval. When she reached the point she saw through the snow a big ship ignorantly bearing straight upon the land. She screamed at her highest pitch, and with frantic energy waved her lantern up and down. The wind blew her voice back—'back into my throat,' she said, 'and almost choked me.' But the light, thank God, was seen, and revealed to the poor mariners in a moment where it was that they really were. Then she had the inexpressible satisfaction of seeing the helm put about, and the ship turned towards the mid-channel. A moment's delay, or the least indecision on the part of the brave little woman, and the good ship would have had her side driven in by the cruel rocks. As they sheered away and blew the fog-horn again, loud and long, she felt that they were thanking their unknown deliverer.

K

CHAPTER XIV

A thousand fantasies
Begin to throng into my memory,
Of calling shapes, and beckoning shadows dire,
And airy tongues that syllable men's names
On sands and shores and desert wildernesses.
                            JOHN MILTON. *Comus.*

CORRIE : *Monday, August 25.*

As our holiday approaches its close we begin to pick up, as it were, things that have been dropped. We remember how many walks that we proposed to take have not been taken ; how many places we intended to visit have remained unvisited. We become economical with our time, and systematic in our arrangements ; this place and that, at any rate, must not be forgotten or overlooked. I suppose it is always so ; in that

North Glen Sannox.

greater span which we call Life, as well as in those short holidays which form a part of it. We begin with prodigality and unthinking exuberance; we end with reflection and a prudent husbandry of what time or opportunity remains to us. In one point the parallel does not hold: if we leave something here unseen, there is a compensation. We hope to come another year; and shall we not see it then? But—the longer journey once finished is finished for ever. Although other and infinite possibilities remain, the chance of return does not appear to be among them.

These thoughts were running through my mind and I gave expression to them. ' Sermonising again,' said a voice beside me.

'Well, isn't it Sunday?' I answered. 'If a man is to be denied his " liberty of prophesying " o' Sundays, what is to become of us?'

This was late in the evening of yesterday, and we were starting for a new walk. While

K 2

rambling about Sannox we had often noticed a
narrow track—narrow, but very distinct—running along the side of that low range of hills
which forms the north-eastern boundary of the
North Glen. It seemed to rise very gradually,
and would give us, we thought, fine inland views,
and then carry us over the ridge and down to
the sea. To this walk, therefore, we bent our
steps. We crossed the North Sannox burn by
the stepping-stones ; and after passing the lonely
shepherd's farm which stands on the brow above,
we turn sharply to the left and find ourselves
among the ruins of an ancient hamlet. It is a
place where a few peasants—shepherds and
fishermen—would naturally come together.
There is shelter from the colder winds, grazing
for sheep on the hill-slopes, and a beautiful river
in the glen beneath, while the sea can be reached
by a path through the wood in a few minutes,
and yet the inhabitants are all gone. I suppose some former lord of the Island drove them

away; and now the roof-trees are broken, the walls have fallen, and the hearths are left cold and bare. Is it not the worst form of sacrilege thus to break in upon the sanctities of human life? Such a place is sadder than a graveyard, and we do not care to linger.

And now the path, which seemed so clear a mile or two away, is by no means easy to find. I have often noticed this. The successive markings, which are so distinct from a distance, can hardly be seen when we stand over them. With a little trouble, however, we get into the track. The turf and the heather have both invaded its lines; but still in most places you may see the wheel-ruts made by the carts of a previous generation. Evidently it started from the now deserted village; but where it went to I cannot imagine, unless, indeed, there was formerly a road running by the hill-side to Loch Ranza instead of, as at present, along the bottom of the valley. The path is well worth traversing for the sake of the new views you get of familiar places. Yonder is our old friend the Cioch-na-h'oighe. My sketch-book already shows a score of separate outlines assumed by this most Protean of peaks; yet here is an entirely different one. From this elevation the peculiar character of the North Glen comes out with great force. It is, as I have already said, somewhat monotonous and melancholy; yet it is full of soft and wide-sweeping lines upon which the eye dwells with pleasure; and beyond, the great hills which look into it but are not of it, present their wildest northern fronts.

When we get near the ridge we find that we have lost the road, so we make straight across and towards the sea. There is not much choice. It is either knee-deep in stiff heather and fern, or ankle-deep in bog and moss. Nor are we sure of our way on the other side; so, as night is coming on, we hasten forward. The declivity

is too steep for a sharp descent; we skirt the
edge, therefore, and presently, coming to some
soft turf, we see that we have worked round
towards the south-easterly end of the chain and
are just above the mouth of the burn from
which we had started.

It is by this time almost dark. The river
near the sea is wide but shallow, and we cross
it. Being now in no doubt as to our homeward
path, we sit down on the shore to take breath.
It is a wild and lonely place. The sea-birds
make strange and half-human noises; the
sound of the advancing tide is sullen and deep;
and over our heads—

> The weak-eyed bat,
> With short shrill shriek flits by on leathern wing.

And what is this that we see on the other side
of the river ? A figure comes out of the dark
wood and walks across the brown spit of sand.
We know by the flow of the dress that it is a
woman. She stands and seems to look wistfully

out to sea. After a while she turns away, as it were sadly, and moves back into the black wood. It is a picture and a mystery. We should like to paint the one and solve the other. We are able to do neither, and I only whisper to my friend :—

> In such a night
> Stood Dido with a willow in her hand,
> Upon the wild sea banks and waft her love
> To come again to Carthage.

The marvellous transparency of the air yesterday was no doubt closely connected with the zone of cloud and storm into which we entered this morning, yet who would have expected that a sunset so hushed and calm would have been closely followed by a sunrise whose accompaniments were heavy rain and violent thunder. The wind, too, had the swing and roar of a tempest.

On the beach I met the Provost, abroad as usual, notwithstanding wind and weather. 'A bad day Provost,' I said.

' Aye, aye, a coorse day—a varra coorse day.'

' The fisher lads will do but poorly.'

' Aye, weel ; the deil's bairns ha' aye their father's luck. And what will *ye* be doing the day ? Ye'll neither get to the taps nor on to the water ; the wind would blaw ye clean aff either o' them. But listen to me the first fair day ye get, gae right onto the taps. Dinna mind your books or your maps, but gae straight oot o' Corrie, and mak for the ridges. Ay man, when ye get there ye'll see the finest sight in a' the Island. Goatfell ? Whew ! it's just a rubble o' stanes, and naething to what ye'll find up there.' I promised to take the old autocrat's advice upon the first opportunity, and pursued my walk in the rain.

In the afternoon there was a great tide. All distant views were hidden. The sky was dark and the sea black, though visited now and then by momentary gleams of silvery light when some cloud was suddenly torn to pieces by the wind.   Going as near to the edge of the rocks as was safe, I stood and watched the grand commotion over which a few white gulls were swooping.   The sea, I observed, had three voices.   First a roar, unceasing, without pause or modulation : that is caused by the multi-tudinous breaking of the waves against each other.   Then a sound of intermittent thunder which results from the flat stroke of a great billow given, now and then, full against the rocks.   And last a heavy rattle like that of musketry which is caused by the tide as it rushes up the beach or drags, more slowly, back again.

During the morning I had been reading that complete text-book of nature and the elements, ' The Prometheus Unbound,' and I could not help noting how fine and true are all the allusions to the ocean.   Nothing here strikes us more than does the ever unbroken sympathy, the trembling resonance which exists between the sky and the sea.   Shelley speaks of the 'Heaven-reflecting sea,' and again of

> The Sea, in storm or calm,
> Heaven's ever-changing Shadow.

His storm-pictures are numerous.   Here is one :—

> Ocean's purple waves,
> Climbing the land, howled to the lashing winds.

And could anything out of Shakespeare be better than this sketch of the sea in calm.   The words are addressed by the Ocean itself to Apollo :—

> My streams will flow
> Round many peopled continents, and round
> Fortunate isles ; and from their glassy thrones
> Blue Proteus and his humid nymphs shall mark
> The shadow of fair ships . . . .
> Borne down the rapid sunset's ebbing sea.

In the evening, although the wind continued, the rain wore itself out ; and, having in mind to make the most of our time, we started for a place on the shore which has the misfortune to be called 'The Fallen Rocks.'   Such names always awaken a prejudice.   We had to pass the

North Burn, and trusted that we should be able
to ford it, as we had done last night.   We found
it, however, quite impassable—swollen by the
storm to a great flood, black in the depths, brown
in the shallows.   Our progress along the shore

"The Islands and the far Shores."

being stopped, we determined to return by the
near bank of the stream.   On that side there is
no path, and we had to force our way through
a thick tangle of birch and hazel, whose grey
stems were all moss-grown.   All the way up to
the bridge the river was a fine sight; sometimes

breaking into a cataract; sometimes rolling over a great boulder with a smooth and oily sweep which only showed how vast was the volume of water; and, at the margin, swirling in and out of the worn rock-basins, just as it must have done for a thousand years. The flood had risen so high that the flowers at the edge of the wood were submerged. We saw a thistle and a hare-bell fighting the current together. The well-rooted thistle looked as if it would live, and held up its head with stubborn bravery; but the poor harebell was as good as lost; it rose and fell, shaking convulsively, and would soon, as could easily be seen, be carried down into the alien tides of the sea.

As we crossed the moor we had a wonderful view of the estuary. The water and the islands beyond were framed by the dense groves of trees which stand on either side of the North Sannox river. Though the clouds were black there was blue in the sky somewhere, or we could not have had that grand deep purple on the stormy sea.

It would have been better if we had then gone straight home. The wild look of the South Glen, however, tempted us; and, in order to look into it, we climbed over the Mid-Sannox ridge. It was an awful sight—a deep cauldron of boiling mist: around it we could just see the grotesque heads of the witch-like mountains looking down upon the 'hell-broth;' and over it the ragged clouds flew like harpies. That was worth going to see. But then, suddenly, the rain swept down once more: and, after hiding for half an hour behind a rock, the dark came down also, and we had to hurry to the bottom with much stumbling and drenching—drenching from below as well as from above. A little further, and a little later, would have resulted in an enforced encampment for the night.

CHAPTER XV

Heigh, my hearts! cheerly, cheerly, my hearts! yare,
yare! Take in the topsail. Tend to the master's whistle.
Blow, till thou burst thy wind, if room enough!

SHAKESPEARE. *The Tempest.*

CORRIE : *Tuesday, August 26.*

AT Corrie there are no yachts. Of this we
have little right to complain : even in Eden
there were omissions. At the same time we had
set our minds upon having at least one short
cruise under canvas ; and, after many protracted
sessions, the boys carried a resolution in favour ·
of our hiring for a day the best and trimmest
trading-smack that we could find. We fixed on
the *Blue Bell* because she was the handsomest
and cleanest-looking craft ; and then we confided
our intentions to Willie M'Niven, the younger

brother of the owner. Willie is the model
boatman of Corrie; so much of a model that
sometimes we can't help laughing at his obvious,
and yet unintentional, resemblance to the Jack-
tar of the stage.   He is splendidly built, muscu-

WILLIE M'NIVEN

lar, and lithe; his head is thickly set with black
curling hair, and his face is both handsome in
form and open in expression.   It would not be
much of an exaggeration to say that he wears
a perennial smile; the difficulty, indeed, is to

catch him when he is not smiling. If you do succeed in coming upon him at a time when he is so far off his guard, the lapse is only momentary. Upon the slightest provocation the smile comes back and spreads over his features, as the sunshine spreads over a green field in April when the light clouds are flying across the sky. He would make his fortune among the London studios, and Poynter or Leighton would find him as useful as Hook. In short, his whole personality is a thing to admire and rejoice in.

With this Adonis of the ocean, then, as I have said, we took counsel and obtained promise of his best help. There were difficulties in the way. The boat was waiting for a favourable opportunity of taking in her cargo of sand and gravel at Sannox, and she might be gone any day; and besides, we must have for our purpose tolerable weather and a fair wind, neither too much nor too little; and then we must know

L

all this the night before, so that the boat might be got ready and brought round. Well, when we came home last night, wet to the skin as a punishment for having dared to look into the Glen at a time when no eye should have been so presumptuous, M'Niven announced to us, greatly to our surprise, that the next day would be fine. The wind had travelled westward with the sun; the bats had been flying about the village; and in other ways it had been announced to him that the morning would be right for our proposed voyage. His forecast was a true one; and this morning, before I was abroad, I heard the boys cheering outside. They had sighted the *Blue Bell* coming round the point out of Sannox Bay. This meant that although the morning was still a doubtful one to us, the seamen knew that the day would be of the right sort.

To victual the ship and get all our numerous party on board was a work of moment. The tide was too low for bringing the *Blue Bell* into harbour, and we had to pull out to her a dozen times with miscellaneous and much-mixed cargoes of provisions and passengers. Then, as there was no convenient ladder, it may be imagined what merriment resulted from the necessary hauling of baskets and ladies up the steep sides of the *Blue Bell*. Of course at the last moment it was found that we had forgotten the corkscrew and the egg-spoons; and once more, therefore, our young crew must return and bring these necessities of over-civilisation. When, finally, one of us, standing at the bow, waved the corkscrew as a signal that our outfit was at length complete, the anchor-chains began to rattle and the assembled *Corriesters* (as we call them), who by this time had gathered to a man round the harbour and stood open-eyed wondering what the mad English would do next, gave a great cheer which echoed from the old quarry behind, and away we went, with a swirl and a dash, shaking out our big brown sails joyously, like a bird preparing for flight.

We made straight across the Sound of Bute, getting fine views, backward, of the receding Arran with its wild granite crown of central peaks; and forward, as we passed, up the wide and stormy frith of Loch Fyne. There was enough wind to give us excitement, and the lads screamed with delight when the *Blue Bell* heeled over so much that standing unassisted was impossible, and, lying on deck, they could almost touch the water with their hands over the gunwale. Going round the east side of the little green islet of Inchmarnock, where the royal fern is still found in great abundance, we came into comparatively calmer water; and spreading our white cloth on deck we gathered round and made a hearty, and, in one sense, an unsteady lunch. We had elected the Critic to be our skipper. The choice was not a random one. His freedom from useless and lubber-like

length of body, his general handiness and rea-
diness, his habit of broadening his base and
hitching his trousers, are all characteristics so
distinctively nautical, that although Art has
claimed him for uses of her own, it is clear that
Nature intended him for the sea. To hear him
' shiver his timbers ' and call for a ' belaying-
pin ' was something famous; but if you had
listened to his singing, with mock heroics, of
Dibdin's ' Drop of the creature,' you would not
soon forget it :—

> Then over life's ocean I'll jog,
>   Let the storm or the Spaniards come on,
> So but sea-room I get and a skin full of grog,
>   I fear neither devil nor Don,
> For I'm the man that's spract and daft,
> In my station amidships, or fore, or aft,
>   I can pull away, cast off, belay,
>   Aloft, alow, avast, yo ho !
>   And hand reef and steer,
>   Know each halliard and jeer,
>   And of duty every rig ;
> But my joy and delight is on Saturday night
>   A drop of the creature to swig.

After lunch the fun became furious. In

latitude 55° 47' the crew mutinied, and sliding
back the hatchway forced the unfortunate
skipper into the hold. He fell softly on a bed
of Sannox sand which had been got in for
ballast, and lay there contented enough, as we
could see through the chinks, until on promise
of another song we gave him his liberty again.
When he stood once more on deck, and, with
his knuckles set upon his hips, ordered us in a
voice of thunder to go ' abaft the binnacle,'
Willie M'Niven and the two other seamen who
were with us laughed till they were like to split.

In the hot afternoon we landed at the
delightful and fairy-looking village of Teigh-na-
bruich, in the Kyles of Bute. Here we laid in
a stock of fruit; and after the lads had bathed,
fearing the wind might drop, we turned southward again and made for home. The Kyles
were at their best, free from mist, as they
should be, and perfect in colour. We went
back by the west shore of Inchmarnock, and

while off there we took our second repast. The
seamen boiled the kettle for us in the little
cabin, and our young gallants showed their
skill by bringing to the ladies brimming cups
of tea, unspilt, across the rolling deck. We
reached Corrie at seven in the evening, and
were welcomed with a salute of good wishes.

Wednesday, August 27.

The weather now seems to alternate day by
day. We have had to-day a wild thundering
sea and heavy rain until evening. At sunset
the tide ran one way and a squall of wind
blew in an opposite direction. The result was
curious. The sea was covered with a shivering
ripple, and the colours of the sky—amber,
bronze, blue, black—were sent shimmering over
the water as if they had been laid on with a
great brush, and were then as suddenly with-
drawn.

Before dark I walked as far as a little

waterfall which is on the hill-side, and yet close by the sea. The day's rain had filled it. It is only some six or eight feet broad, but the falls of Tempe could not have been lovelier. It runs over a sloping slab of grey rock and then tumbles into a pool. On each side grows a white-stemmed mountain ash. These meet above, and from them depend the sprays of a honeysuckle ten feet in length, which sway backwards and forwards in the wind, as if they were toying with the waterfall, their playfellow. A few yards downward and this fall reaches the sea; a few yards upward and over the fern-covered shoulder of the hill appears the purple peak of Cioch-na-h'oighe. In this sylvan nook I have spent many musing hours; and no wonder, for here in one tiny plot the mountain and the sea, the woodland and the waterfall, unite their varied charms.

CHAPTER XVI

Oh, 'twas an unimaginable sight !
Clouds, mists, streams, watery rocks and emerald turf,
Clouds of all tincture, rocks and sapphire sky,
Confused, commingled, mutually inflamed,
Molten together, and composing thus,
Each lost in each, that marvellous array
Of temple, palace, citadel, and huge
Fantastic pomp of structure without name,
In fleecy folds voluminous, enwrapped.
                    WORDSWORTH. *The Excursion*, Book II.

CORRIE : *Thursday, August* 28.

To-DAY we have made our projected excursion along the mountain ridges. The morning was a doubtful one, and the Provost, when appealed to, shook his head, and declined to commit himself either on one side or the other. 'Shrewd old Scot,' I said, as I turned indoors, leaving him on the sward outside, with his face turned to the sky, and veering round like a weathercock. 'Shrewd old Scot'; one need not give you the well-worn advice of Esquire Biglow's gran'ther—

Don't never prophesy,—onless ye know.

A single glance at the Ordnance Survey of Arran will show why a scramble along the ridges should be especially interesting. The great mountains are all in the northern half of the island. South of Brodick Bay, the coast is fine enough; although the inland hills are comparatively low, the highest being not more than about 1,600 feet, and many of them only 800 or 900 feet; but in the region which lies north of a line running from Brodick on the east coast to Mauchrie on the west, you find all the loftiest, grandest, and most rugged peaks. Bryce, in his 'Geology of Arran,' divides these peaks into three groups. Let us look at them on the map. First there is the Ben Bharrain group. This runs roughly parallel with the west coast, and is divided from the other two by the long and deep valleys called Glen Iorsa and Glen Eas-an-Bhiarach. On the eastern side of these glens there is first the Cior-Mhor group; and further east again—fronting, in fact, the eastern shore—there is the Goatfell group. It is in these two last that the peculiarity to which I wish to draw attention is most clearly evident. The map shows it in a moment. All the numerous peaks are connected, we observe, by singularly continuous ridges, and the two groups are also united by a low ridge or *col*. You do not, therefore, need to descend from one summit into a valley and then to climb again ; but once on the heights you might, as it seems to me, travel about for days and visit every peak without once coming back to the valleys. Of these two eastern ranges, Cior-Mhor is the pivot or centre ; and from it irregular curving or angular lines radiate to

north, south, and east in so striking and fantastic a manner, that an appearance is presented such as I have not seen on any other
map than that of Arran.

The morning, as I have said, was doubtful;
but, after waiting until about eleven o'clock, we
determined to start.   The wind was in the
south-west, and very strong.   Both sky and sea
were blue—full of dash and freedom, the white
clouds flying at lightning speed across the one,
and the foam-spray rising like smoke from the
other.   We begin the ascent from our own
garden-wall and go straight for Am-Binnein.
Up, over the flowery slopes of turf and through
the birch copses; then across the old sea-level,
a wild and desolate plain at a height of 600
feet; and, following a steep water-course, we
reach the depressed lip of the hollow or basin
which is right over Corrie.   If it were not for
this depression facing the sea the hollow would
contain a tarn, for the ridge runs almost entirely

round it. Turning now a little to the left we
begin to climb the front of Am-Binnein, which
consists of great rock-slabs piled precipitously
one upon another. We pause often to take
breath. Far below we see the steamer coming
into Corrie. She looks like a tiny toy moving
across the blue. The fierce wind is against her,
and we observe how she has to curve round in
order to reach the black dot which means the
ferry boat. We know on good authority that
bees—

> Soar for. bloom,
> High as the highest Peak of Furness-fells—

yet we are surprised to find here, at an elevation
of 1,400 feet, a solitary bee fighting with the
wind. At twelve o'clock the sky lowers, and,
although the wind continues, rain begins to fall.
We know now that our hope of fine weather is
gone; but, having resolved to go forward, we
creep behind the rocks and wait till the shower
abates.

We are now at the height of about 1,600 feet; and, looking north-east by east, there comes into view the most glorious rainbow which it has ever been our fortune to behold. We do not look up to it, but down upon it; and its marvellously intense colours are painted not upon the background of the sky, but upon the sea and the land. Its southern limb, which is upon our right, touches the very hill on which we stand; then it curves close by the Corrie landing creek, runs out as far as Garroch Head, returns by North Sannox, and, finally, rests its northern base on a point of the hill-range not far to the left of us. Having described quite seven-eighths of a circle it should hardly, perhaps, be called a bow. It was worth the trouble of climbing on to this craggy shelf if only to see so wonderful a spectacle beneath us and around us; and, as we look at it, we think of that unsurpassed vision of the Ancient of Days, and of the rainbow-encircled throne in the Apocalypse.

When the rain-cloud has passed over we begin to climb again, slowly and painfully, over the great blocks ; and ever the wind gets more and more fierce. At length we are on the ridge, which now rises very gradually to the summit of Am-Binnein. If the day were calm we could pass along this ridge as easily as along the high-road on the beach 2,100 feet below; but now the blast from the south-west is terrible, and we are obliged to creep along the hill-side just below the ridge, so that the wind drives us against the mountain. If we were on the top the chances are that it would blow us over ; and we know that the other or northern side is precipitous. Coming to a place where there is a grassy hollow, we venture to stand up and look around us. We can barely keep upon our feet. My friend, making a trumpet of his hands, shouts to me—' This is a new experience.' ' Precisely '—but before I have time to give that answer, I am on my back. The wind has flung

me, as an expert wrestler would fling an assail-
ant, with one throw flat upon the ground.
After that we become still more cautious, not
knowing what goblin pranks may be played
with us ; but more than once we are seized, as
if by demoniacal possession, shaken in every
limb, and blown to the earth. At length we
curl ourselves up behind a great stone in order
to get breath enough to speak to each other,
and also that we may watch the wild hurly-
burly of the elements which is going on before
us. We look down now into the great hollow
under Goatfell, whose summit is directly south-
west. The wind is driving up from the sea vast
masses of cloud and vapour; they strike the
rampart of Goatfell, and then, torn into a
hundred shreds by their contact with the rocks,
come streaming round at inconceivable speed as
though they were flying from their tormentor
like the 'scourged souls' in Malebolge, the
eighth circle of the 'Inferno,' that place—

> Within the depths of hell
> Of rock dark-stained . . . .
> With hue ferruginous, e'en as the steep
> That round it circling winds.

Some of these fragmentary cloudlets sink exhausted into the gulf; others, more fiercely driven, cross over and strike us in the face, even as Dante says :—

> Below
> Were naked sinners. Hitherward they came,
> Meeting our faces, from the middle point.

From this place we pursued our way along the ridges in a south-westerly direction towards the base of the Goatfell Peak. Here we get partial protection from the wind. The clouds are ever shifting and the views are of the grandest character. Suddenly we see the *col* or saddle which connects the range on which we are standing with that of Cior-Mhor, and along which we are intending to travel; then we recognise by its torrent-seams and its rock-markings Cior-Mhor itself; and Suidhe-Fergus; and the South Sannox Glen, with its burn, first

M

a mere thread running in the green bog or moss, and then a wider stream with banks of white pebble or sand. And now a descending cloud blots out everything, and while we stand amazed at the change, lo ! we see in the north-

The Saddle and Cir Mhor

east a break, no bigger, as it seems, than a man's hand, and through it there comes, as a picture, Loch Ranza in the colours of bright sunlight, and looking like a glimpse of some other world than that on which we stand. After this there is again a partial clearing of the sky, and we get sight of the sea beyond North Sannox, and of the hills near to it, the latter being clothed in that wondrous aerial tint which is a mixture of grey, purple, and green, and which no man knows better how to paint than our old friend Clarence Whaite.

As we are descending the crags westward in search of the saddle a dark mist falls, and with it comes the rain. We can hardly see a foot before us, and dare not proceed. We are crag-bound, and creep into a narrow crevice for shelter. It is bitterly cold; and when we can stand still no longer, we come out of our hiding-place and pace about like sentries over the few feet of level ground that is available. Every instant there is some faint change, and the crags around us alternate in colour from black to grey. These crags are of the most fantastic shapes, and the mist works witchery upon them. We see all sorts of things—cowled monks, gargoyle heads with portentous noses, Don

Quixote and Sancho Panza, and all the beasts
on Ararat, walking in grotesque procession. In
this durance we spend a full hour, and then,
being thoroughly cold and wet, my companion's
store of caloric is exhausted, and we are compelled to move. It would be madness to go
forward ; but fortunately, having kept our
reckoning as to the points of the compass, we
are able to retreat by the way we came.
Unwillingly, therefore, we begin our return ;
and, carefully noting each point, we grope our
way back to the great hollow which is between
Am-Binnein and Goatfell. We had remarked
that in the extreme north-western corner, where
the soil was very red, there was a good descent
and no precipices. To this, therefore, we make
our way with much deliberation. Having
found it, we rattle down without fear. When
we have descended about five hundred feet we
leave the mist behind us ; and, though the rain
continues, it is clear over the sea, and we can

make out the pink line of the coast and the white huts of High Corrie.

As we are crossing the old sea-level we startle a fine red buck. He goes scouring across the heather, and we are delighted with his splendid spring and carriage. At half-past five we reach the bottom wet and weary, but longing for the opportunity of another day upon the ridges.

After tea we heard that a stag had been shot by one of the Duke's relatives, and was lying in the School-house yard. We went out to look at him, and were saddened to find · that it was the noble fellow whom we ourselves had roused. He had been shot right through the breast. We felt like mourners when we saw him lifted into a cart and driven off to the Castle.

Late at night there is an awful sea. The tide has risen to the level of the rocks, and the waves come swirling over into the road. At the harbour there is an exciting scene; the boats are in danger, and all the men are out; and, in the midst of it all, a strange lighter runs in for shelter. It was her only chance. If she had not been successful, the seamen say, she must certainly have foundered in the night.

CHAPTER XVII

The holidays were fruitful, but must end ;
One August evening had a cooler breath ;
Into each mind intruding 'duties crept ;
Under the cinders burned the fires of home ;
Nay, letters found us in our Paradise ;
So in the gladness of the new event
We struck our camp, and left the happy hills.

RALPH WALDO EMERSON. *The Adirondacs.*

CORRIE : *Friday, August* 29.

THE weather continues wild and broken, but sunlight predominates over rain ; and during the morning I have counted more than a dozen rainbows gleaming over the sea. Some are complete, some are in segments, one or two have been double and very brilliant, but none, of course, have equalled the splendid circle seen from the mountain-side yesterday. The most

curious thing has been the way in which, as a
result of mingling rain and wind and cloud and
sun, they have appeared and disappeared—a
fragment here, a fragment there—producing
such an effect of wild beauty as it is quite
impossible to describe. I know of no other
appearance which, precisely in the same way,
seems to lift the earth out of its prosaic round,
making it, at once, the companion and the
subject of ethereal powers.

In the evening I go a-fishing with one of
my boys in the Corrie burn. We put forth all
our poor skill, making most persevering casts
in the shallows and in the deeps, under the big
stones and where the boughs of oak and birch
make a dark shade, but the trout will not rise.
Probably it is too late for them, and I walk
on alone up the bank of the stream, and then
turn into the hamlet of High Corrie. This
place stands on a little plateau a few hundred
feet up the mountain. It is older than the

village below, and the huts are of the true
Highland type—long, low, white, thick-walled,
and heavily bonneted with thatch. Some people
prefer to lodge here; the air is certainly invigorating, but to me there is always a per-

High Corrie

ceptible touch of melancholy. The black mountains are too near. One feels this, of course,
more strongly on an evening like the present,
when the sky is dark and monotonous. Suddenly, however, the dulness is broken, as so
often happens just at sunset, the heavy clouds

take a blue tinge, the sea turns red, and a crimson pennon of vapour is hung out for a few minutes from the topmost rock-turret of Cioch-na-h'oighe, as if for signal that the day is ended.

The twilight is coming on fast as I make my way back again towards the burn. I am walking with my eyes turned to the ground when I am conscious of a new radiance in the air. Has the sunlight come back again? I lift up my head, and—there is the moon. She has risen stealthily, under cover of the clouds, and now for a moment through a narrow rift she pours down upon the sea a sudden flood of mellow light.

Sunday, August 31.

Yesterday we had again a lively breeze. In the morning we made a run along the coast in a lug-sail, but the amusement was too exciting. As we passed each mountain gorge the wind came down with such uncertain puffs that our amateur sailors were perplexed, and we were glad to get into harbour again.

In the afternoon we went to Brodick. The annual sports were being held there, in the bay and on the shore under the Castle. The Duke was going about among the people, and some of his guests were competing for prizes. In the middle of what is called a 'duck-hunt' there came on a storm of thunder and rain which rather dashed the sports, but which did not prevent us from making a pleasant detour homeward through the grand pine-woods which lie below the Castle, and are enclosed within its grounds.

When the Corrie men reached home at night with their boat, which had done good service against the men of Brodick and Lamlash, we gave them an ovation at the quay. Willie M'Niven came up smiling, of course—came up, one would say, rather, as an embodied smile. You should have seen his magnificent chest when he rolled back his white guernsey and bent himself to the oar in the final race at Brodick. Before we turned in, the wind had got round to the north, and there was grand, clear moonlight and a brilliant star, with a measurable disk, rising over the sea.

This morning we had to acknowledge to ourselves, somewhat sadly, that our last day had come. Sadness, however, was not long compatible with such a scene as we had before us. The wind was north-west, the sky gloriously blue, and chequered with white clouds; the sea purple; and the Lesser Cumbrae, which is far away across the Firth of Clyde, so clear that its curious terraces of trap-rock were as distinct as if they had only been distant a mile or two. Before breakfast we had our usual dip, and enjoyed greatly the roughness of the water. The wind was very high, and Master Fred's shirt was blown into the sea. Outside there would have been danger; but within the creek we could afford to play with the big waves that came racing up and then sprang headlong over the rocky barrier behind which we were waiting for them.

As we walked slowly along the road, in the middle of the forenoon, on our way to the quiet little kirk, we found ourselves dwelling upon every feature of the place with a tenderness which implied an impending farewell. The sea, the sky, the woods, are full of gladsome life and motion. The deep blue water is dotted now all over with white waves, which come dancing in from what is always to me the joyous north; the sun is hot, though the wind is cool; the anchored boats toss in the harbour; and the cattle, with an evident sense of pleasure, are feeding on the grassy margin of the tide.

In the evening, as there will be now no other opportunity, two of us start for the Fallen Rocks. The walk is a familiar one as far as the wooden bridge over the South Sannox burn.

This we cross, then, passing the kirk, we go down to the shore. When we reach the mouth of the North burn the sun has disappeared behind the western hills; but the vast open sky, east of us and above the water, is made magnificent by clouds which reflect the colours of sunset. Then the moon, pale and supernaturally large, is detected hanging low down over the far-off hills of Ayr. We cross the burn by the stepping-stones, and pursue our solitary way along the shore. It is a wonderfully fine piece of coast scenery—very wild and lonely. From this point it would be a nine or ten miles' walk to Loch Ranza, following the sea, and nowhere, if I remember rightly, should we come upon a human habitation. On one side is the water; on the other, and very near, a range of hills—Torr Reamhar, Crogan, Laggan, Creag Ghlas, and Torr Meadhonach. These hills are rock-crowned, decked with heather, or dark with hanging woods. The path beneath them is broken and uncertain, sometimes on the turf, sometimes on the sand, and now through beds of bracken which are five or six feet high. At about two miles from Sannox we reach the scene which is known as the Fallen Rocks. As you come nearer a feeling of wonder deepens into something very nearly akin to horror. High above, you see where, in some wild convulsion, half the mountain front has fallen away, and then rolled in vast blocks, like a torrent of stone, down to the shore. Some of these huge lumps of rock would weigh over a thousand tons each, and there are hundreds of them. The foremost have reached the water, consequently they bar the path, and you have to climb over them. The shells and the festooning weeds tell you where it is that the sea frequently reaches. Nor is it difficult to imagine what the spectacle must be with a full tide on stormy nights in winter, when the howling waves will rush over the rocks and boil with fury in the labyrinth of holes and passages among them.

Immediately beyond the rocks, which form a kind of headland, there is a delightful cove in which the water is clear and still, and the sand clean, smooth, and free from stones. By this time the twilight is almost gone, and the full moon, followed by the evening star, has become resplendent. Just now she is behind a small but thick cloud, and is raining down a plenitude of light upon the sea. The place and the hour are both enchanted, and we say to each other, 'No man, at any time since ever the world began, could possibly have seen anything, in its kind, more lovely than this.'

Although, in our return, we have full moonlight along the shore, we find the North Glen and its burn lying in deep shadow. It is too dark to cross the stepping-stones, and we follow the right bank of the stream in order to find

Birds on the shore. Bredick. Bay

the bridge. Near the shepherd's house we lose the path, and while we are beating about for the bridge we hear familiar voices calling. After a little trouble we come together, and then find that our young people with all their friends—a goodly company—have come out from the village to meet us. Having found the bridge we linger there, pensive yet well-pleased, looking up to the dark mountains or down upon the shadowy stream. It was our last night. We must needs celebrate it, therefore, with Sabbath songs of the country, and the shepherd in his lonely hut might well have wondered what spirits were abroad when he heard—

> Dundee's wild warbling measures rise,
> Or plaintive Martyrs, worthy of the name.

Monday, September 1.

At half-past four we are up and out of doors. The sun is rising behind the purple hills that lie beyond the Frith. The sky is amber and

N

crimson; but the strangest thing is the shore.
That is still deep black; but the pools left by
the receding tide are bright as silver. At six
o'clock, after many tender adieux, we have
begun our homeward journey, and are driving
along the road to catch the steamer at Brodick.
The morning is fine and clear. We see the
porpoises rolling in the blue water; the hares
are frisking across the highway; the deer
scamper through the wood when the coachman
cracks his whip, and the pair of herons which
have their nest in the high beeches near the
Castle are standing, as usual, on a big stone
by the edge of the sea.

And so ends the story of our pleasant holiday in Arran, of whose shores we take farewell
in the words of a poet-friend (from whom I
have already quoted), who, although he knows
intimately some of the best scenery in Europe,
has abated nothing of his admiration for the
wonderfully varied Island in the Clyde.

Arran, I thought of thee indeed as fair,
  But all that fancy feigned the fact excels :
  Not that Atlantis of which Plato tells,
Nor isles of Sirens in the southern air,
From British Arran beauty's prize would bear.
  Above, dark peaks, lone glens, and crystal wells ;
  Below, the cottaged slopes, the brick-clad swells,
And ocean's voice for ever sounding there.

Farewell, a sad farewell, beloved land !
  And other hearts to peaceful dreams beguile ;
Still in my thought thy cloven peaks shall stand,
  Still wave thy fringing forests fair, that smile
O'er lovelier seas than wash the Italian strand,
  Or marbled cape of an Ionian isle.

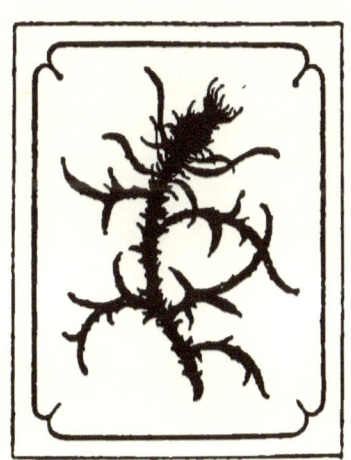

INDEX OF QUOTATIONS

MISCELLANEOUS NOTES

PAGE 1.

Arran. The Island of Arran lies in the Estuary of the Clyde between Cantire and the coast of Ayr. It is most easily reached by Ardrossan, from which port it is distant about twelve miles. The most convenient landing-place is Brodick. The island is some twenty miles long by twelve broad. It is remarkable for the great variety which it presents in so small an area. This applies to its geology as well as to the character of its scenery. Byrce, in his ' Arran and other Clyde Islands,' says, ' The number of rock-formations, sedimentary and plutonic, which are found within this limited space is truly remarkable, perhaps unparalleled in any tract of like extent on the surface of the globe; while the varied phenomena which they present in their mutual contacts and general relations to one another are of the highest import in theoretical geology.' Speaking generally, the eastern side of the island is most interesting, and the finest mountain scenery will be found in a tract of country of which Cior Mhor and Goatfell are the central points and which includes the two noble glens of Sannox and Rosa.

PAGE 1.

Corrie. The hamlet of Corrie is six miles north of Brodick. The Glasgow or Greenock steamers, which come by Rothesay, call at Corrie, but there is no pier, and the landing is made in boats. Conveyances run frequently from Brodick. The hotel is smaller than the one at Brodick, but is eminently comfortable.

PAGE 28.

The Holy Island is a mountain islet lying off the village of Lamlash. Its height is about a thousand feet. It takes its name from having been the legendary residence of Molios, an Irish saint of the sixth century.

PAGE 68.

The Castle at Loch Ranza is a fine object, whether seen from the sea with the mountains as a background, or from the village with the sea behind it. Though roofless, a considerable portion is still standing. It was a hunting-seat and a royal castle so far back as 1380.

PAGE 103.

Graveyard of St. Michael. An ancient cemetery on the left hand of the lane leading into Glen Sannox. A chapel formerly stood here, dedicated to St. Michael. Near the gate, and built into the low stone wall, may still be seen an almost obliterated image of the saint. The little cluster of graves, surrounded by the Sannox mountains, make a solemn and touching picture.

PAGE 132.

A deserted hamlet. It is said that a large population formerly inhabited the North Glen, but that in 1832 five hundred persons were induced or compelled to leave the island. They were furnished with means of reaching New Brunswick, and formed a settlement there at Chaleur Bay.

PAGE 175.

The Fallen Rocks. According to Headrick, the disruption occurred about 1707. 'Immense masses,' he says, 'fell from these rocks, and now encumber the beach, rendering it difficult and dangerous to pass along the shore. The concussion shook the earth, and the sound was heard in Bute and Argyleshire.'

PAGE 178.

Herons. There is a superstition in the Island that the prosperity of the Dukes of Hamilton is connected with continued existence of these herons, and it is said they are carefully preserved. The old people shake their heads and say, 'Ah, well; when the herons are gone the Dukes o' Hamilton will be gone too.'

PRINTED BY
SPOTTISWOODE AND CO., NEW-STREET SQUARE
LONDON